A Million Miles from Boston

A Million Miles from Boston

KAREN DAY

WENDY
LAMB
BOOKS

Text copyright © 2011 by Karen Day
Jacket art copyright © 2011 by Miles Hyman

All rights reserved. Published in the United States by Wendy Lamb Books, an imprint of Random House Children's Books, a division of Random House, Inc., New York.

Wendy Lamb Books and the colophon are trademarks of Random House, Inc.

Visit us on the Web! www.randomhouse.com/kids

Educators and librarians, for a variety of teaching tools, visit us at
www.randomhouse.com/teachers

Library of Congress Cataloging-in-Publication Data
Day, Karen.
A million miles from Boston / Karen Day. — 1st ed.
p. cm.
Summary: Rising seventh-grader Lucy plans on a perfect summer at the Maine lake where her family has owned a cottage for decades, but family of a classmate she dislikes has bought a home there and her widowed father is bringing a girlfriend to visit.
ISBN 978-0-385-73899-6 (hc) — ISBN 978-0-385-90763-7 (lib. bdg.) —
ISBN 978-0-375-89690-3 (ebook) [1. Vacation homes—Fiction.
2. Summer—Fiction. 3. Single-parent families—Fiction. 4. Friendship—Fiction.
5. Dogs—Fiction. 6. Family life—Maine—Fiction. 7. Maine—Fiction.] I. Title.
PZ7.D3316Mil 2011
[Fic]—dc22
2010016475

Printed in the United States of America

10 9 8 7 6 5 4 3 2 1

First Edition

For Jeane
And for Emma and Rebecca

Chapter 1

Ian Richards walked around the corner of the nature exhibit at the mall, his long arms swinging. He had thick blond hair and a smirk on his face.

"Wanna see what I found?" He glanced at us: me, Annie, Rachel and Mei. Ian was one of the most popular boys in our grade, but he didn't like me. I didn't like him, either. "Come on," he said. "Follow me."

Mei turned to me. "Lucy, come on!"

My friends and I were celebrating the end of sixth grade, two weeks away. We'd had a great day, shopping and getting our ears pierced. I glanced across the mall to the restaurant where the moms sat talking. I'd much rather have gone back to them, but Annie, Rachel and Mei had already started after Ian.

Charlie and Michael, two boys from our grade, stood near the exhibit.

"Let's be quick," Mei whispered. Like me, she was kind of shy around boys.

"Look! Think they're real?" Ian pointed to turtles on a long, flat rock next to a small pond.

"Cute," Annie said. "But fake. They're not moving."

Trees, grass, bushes and pond took up the whole center of the mall. Water fell in a long, straight line from a boulder high above us, and the air was warm and damp. The birch trees had perfect branches with soft, shiny green leaves. I touched the white bark. Plastic.

Ian grinned and climbed over a low fence into the exhibit.

"What are you doing?" Annie tried to grab his shirt. "Someone'll see you!"

Ian squatted in front of a turtle. "Are you real?"

"Dude!" Michael laughed.

A sign read KEEP OUT. DO NOT FEED FISH OR TURTLES.

I looked around. A man sat on a nearby bench, reading. A little girl watched us from across the pond. She looked about seven, the same age as my brother, Bucky. Her mom bent over a stroller.

I turned back to Ian. We hadn't talked since we were paired for the water project the past winter. What a disaster.

Ian dropped to his hands and knees and lowered his face to the turtle. It was the size of my palm and it stared back at him, neck, face and limbs still. Then Ian rounded his back, pinched his lips into an O and sucked in his cheeks, making his eyes small.

"Be careful or the turtle'll think you're his mother," Charlie said. Everyone cracked up, even me. He *did* look like a turtle.

"Hey, you alive?" Ian poked the turtle's shell. Its head and limbs popped into its shell. Ian startled and sat back.

Michael laughed. "You afraid of a little turtle?"

Ian grabbed the turtle and jumped out of the exhibit. He thrust it at Annie. "Killer turtle! Gonna eat you!"

Annie and Rachel screamed and ran behind Charlie. Ian shoved the turtle in Mei's face but she just put her hands on her hips and scowled. He went after Annie and Rachel, waving the turtle in front of him as if it were a weapon.

"Eew! Get that away from me!" Annie screamed.

"Killer turtle!" Ian lifted the turtle over his head, then zoomed it down at me.

I stared at the turtle, only inches from my nose. It had to be terrified, dizzy, maybe hurt. I glanced at the little girl who watched, her lips quivering.

"Stop it!" I said. "You're scaring the turtle!"

Ian turned it to face him. "Turtles don't feel."

I yelled, "How would you like it if someone swung *you* around that way? Of course he can feel. He disappeared inside his shell!"

"Oh, so you're an expert on turtles, *too*?" Ian glared at me.

"You two aren't going to start fighting again, are you?" Annie asked.

Ian and I had gotten into a big argument during the water

project after he had pulled up a photo of a naked man on our librarian's computer and blamed it on me.

"Miss Perfect Student!" Now Ian grinned at the others.

"God, Ian," Mei said. Then she added, "So annoying," under her breath.

"We gotta go," Charlie said. "Just put the turtle back."

I walked up close to Ian. How would he like it if I called *him* a name?

I glanced at the little girl watching, then down at the turtle. Its shell was beautiful, with different shades of brown and black and white speckles. I lowered my voice. "See that little girl? She's scared. Let me have the turtle so she doesn't have nightmares about this. Okay?"

I hadn't planned to say this and Ian seemed as surprised as I was. He let me take the turtle.

I climbed into the exhibit and set the turtle next to the water. I waited, but its body stayed inside its shell.

"Lucy! What are you *doing?*" Mei's mom walked up.

"I was just . . ." I stood and looked at my friends.

"You shouldn't be in there!" Mrs. Wu said.

"Shame on you, Lucy Goosey! Breaking the rules again!" Ian laughed.

"What?" I glared at him.

"It's your fault!" Mei said to Ian.

He grinned and stuck out his hand toward Mrs. Wu. "Ian Richards. Nice to meet you."

They shook and Mrs. Wu said, "What's going on here?"

Ian laughed, knocked off Michael's cap and grabbed it

from the ground. Then he ran toward the stores, Charlie and Michael following.

Ian had done it again, blamed something he'd done on me!

Mei told her mom what had happened. Mrs. Wu said, "I'm sorry I was cross, Lucy. I didn't know the whole story. Girls, we're leaving in ten minutes. Make sure you wash your hands, Lucy. We'll wait at the restaurant."

"He's such a jerk," Rachel said.

"True," Annie said. "But he's funny, don't you think? And kinda cute?"

"Annie!" I said. Everyone laughed.

They walked over to a nearby store. I looked across the pond. The little girl was gone and the turtle remained inside its shell.

Sometimes my black lab, Superior, and I saw turtles in the woods at Pierson Point, Maine, where my family and I spent summers. Thinking of the Point made me happy. Who cared about Ian? Soon I'd be up there.

"Lucy, come on," Mei called.

"Okay." The turtle's head inched out of its shell, and I smiled and ran off to wash my hands.

When I got back, the moms were still talking at their table.

My mom had died years earlier, so I was used to being on my own. But I really liked that my friends' moms were always nice to me.

I raised my hand to my ear and twisted my new stud. The

saleswoman had told us to do that twice a day to keep our ears from getting infected.

"Don't our ears look *fab?*" Annie asked. Everybody laughed and agreed.

Earlier, when we had gotten our ears pierced, each mom had stood by her daughter, taking pictures, clapping. When it was my turn, all three moms crowded around me.

"You're ready for middle school," Mrs. Stein said.

In two weeks we'd be done with Taylor Elementary, forever. Exciting. Scary, too.

But one good thing to look forward to: in the big new middle school, I could get away from Ian Richards.

Chapter 2

Taylor Elementary was named after Jack Taylor, a hero in World War II who had been from our neighborhood. My brother, Bucky, thought that was cool and he loved to talk about it with our dad, who taught history at a college.

But what I liked most about Taylor were the people.

Every morning our principal greeted us at the door. My first-grade teacher gave me hugs when I saw her. And Mrs. Jonas, the best librarian in the world, looked the other way when I was late returning my favorite Audubon book, *Birds of America*.

I knew that the gym teacher set up the obstacle course in the fall, the art teacher taught pastels in the spring and the lunch lady made extra brownies on Tuesdays. Sometimes teachers retired and new ones were hired. Sometimes they switched classrooms or taught different grades. But mostly Taylor was the same year after year.

I thought about that as I looked out the window of the bus at Duggan Middle School. It had been nearly a week since we had pierced our ears. Since then, our class had sung in its last concert and had its end-of-the-year picnic.

That day we'd toured Duggan. It was brand new and huge— four elementary schools fed into it—with three wings, a five-hundred-seat auditorium and a cafeteria so big you could barely see across it. The teachers we met were busy, official. And there were many of them.

"You'll get into a routine next year and then it won't be so new," Jenny, our babysitter, had said that morning as I'd stared at my uneaten toast. She grinned. "You're such a creature of habit."

"Is that bad?"

"No, silly."

Now Annie and Rachel bounced into the seat in front of me.

"Wasn't it awesome?" Annie said. "Finally! My cousin in Rhode Island has been in middle school since fifth grade."

Our class had stayed in elementary school an extra year, until Duggan was completed.

"Did you see the cafeteria?" Rachel asked. "This is *way* cool!"

"Yeah." I swallowed.

Charlie and Michael dove into the seat in front of Annie and Rachel. Everyone laughed and talked. I smiled. Duggan *was* cool. How come I wasn't excited? Was I the only one who felt this way?

A paper wad sailed over my head. When I looked up, Ian stood next to me.

Ever since the day at the mall, we'd ignored each other. Now he stared at me, his hands jammed in his sweatshirt pockets, his freckles scrunched on his nose. I squeezed my knees. Was he going to sit here? Say something?

Then someone pushed him from behind and he moved on. I let go of my knees as Mei ran down the aisle and sat next to me.

The bus driver pulled away as she said, "What'd you think?"

"It's pretty big."

"Huge." She tucked her black hair behind her ears. "I'm kinda dreading it."

I whipped my head to look at her. I'd known Mei since kindergarten. We were part of a big group of kids who went to each other's birthday parties and played on the same soccer teams. This year Mei, Annie, Rachel and I had become best friends. But we'd never really talked about anything too serious.

"Why?" I asked.

"I got lost. A custodian had to take me to the principal's office. My first day and I was already in the principal's office. I'm terrible at directions. And I'm *so* dreading seventh-grade math. It's supposed to be super hard."

"I guess we'll have to study harder, right?"

She nodded, eyes down.

I looked out the window. I wasn't worried about math or getting lost. "I wish we could stay at Taylor."

"Me too."

We smiled at each other.

I sat up. "Don't worry about the first day. I'll walk with you to your first class. And I'll help you with math, too. It's gotta be easier if we work together."

"Okay, thanks." She smiled, more broadly this time.

I was glad to help. But what could Mei do about my worries? I couldn't stay in sixth grade forever.

When I walked into my house, I heard Superior barking, her nails clicking as she ran down the stairs and into my arms.

"I missed you, too." I sat on the kitchen floor. Superior, licking my face, tried to get into my lap, but she was too big and fell out. I laughed, turned her over and scratched her tummy as she swished her tail on the floor. I stood.

"Well?" Jenny walked into the kitchen. When Dad had hired her, she had been a graduate student at the college where he taught and was only supposed to be our babysitter until she graduated. But that had been six years earlier and she was still with us. She was still a graduate student, too.

"It was okay." I loved talking to Jenny, but I just wanted to forget about that day. Superior barked again and tried to wiggle between my legs. I scratched her back.

"She's been looking for you for hours." Jenny opened a cabinet and started putting food into a big box on the counter. I peeked inside—tomato soup, chicken noodle soup, pasta, canned tomatoes.

I grinned. Moving up to Pierson Point for the summer was the best part of the year and it was only days away.

But it was a little sad, too. Every summer we went to the Point and Jenny went back to her family's dairy farm in Wisconsin. We didn't see each other for two months.

"I'll miss you," I said.

"Me too." She held out her arms and I sank into her big tummy. "I've got a surprise for you."

I pulled away. The week before, after Rachel had a surprise party, I begged Jenny never to throw a party like that for me. Rachel's party was okay, but I saw her panic when everyone yelled, "Surprise!" I like knowing what's going to happen.

"Don't worry," Jenny said, laughing. "It's just dinner. Burritos, your favorite."

"Thanks," I said. "Where's Dad?"

"He's having dinner with Julia."

The hairs on the back of my neck stood up. At first Dad had called her his physical therapist, when she'd treated him for his sore back the year before. By the time I met her, three months ago, it was just "Julia." I thought of her as "the PT."

"Why?"

"You're headed to the Point soon. He probably wants to say good-bye."

I reached for Superior, who licked my hand.

Good-bye to the PT. Good riddance. See you next fall. Or if we were lucky, never again.

"Why don't you take Superior out before she splits a gut?" Jenny said.

Outside, Superior trotted to the bushes. We'd adopted her not long after Mom had died. Dad had gotten her from a friend; she was a reject from a guide dog program, because she carried a gene that might cause her to go blind. I'd been in my room the afternoon Dad had brought her home, and I remembered lifting my head off my pillow to look at her.

She was the most beautiful thing I'd ever seen. Silky black, big eyes, big smile.

All day I played with her, showing her the house and walking her around the block. That night she slept on the rug next to my bed, and the next day I taught her to fetch the newspaper and pee in the grass behind the garage.

Dad couldn't believe how quickly she learned. Jenny said she was "far superior" to any dog she'd ever known, and the name stuck.

I couldn't always remember what had happened to me when I was younger. But whenever I asked Jenny if my memories of Superior from those first two days were right, she said, "That's exactly how it happened. And she's been *your dog* ever since."

I sat in the grass near Superior. Our yard was tiny, the nearby houses crammed close. We lived in Boston, with shops and buildings at the end of our street. A stop for the T, our subway, was just around the corner.

Once, I'd seen a hawk in Boston, but mostly all I saw were people. The Point had ducks, geese, seals, cormorants, foxes, crabs, turtles, raccoons. The year before, Dad had seen an eagle. Up there the sky was big and clear, with so many stars that at night you hardly needed a flashlight. And all day long, you could go without shoes or socks. Everyone kept their cottage doors unlocked, windows open.

The screen door creaked and Jenny stuck her head out. "I was thinking. Might be nice for you all to have visitors up to the Point this summer. Don't you think?"

Visitors? Occasionally a friend of Dad's came up. But there was so much to do, so many old friends already there. And I loved keeping our lives at the Point separate from our lives here. But then I had a thought: maybe Mei could come before she went to sleepaway camp. She'd love it!

"I think Julia is okay, Lucy," Jenny said. "I feel it in my bones."

I stroked Superior. Thinking about the PT turned my stomach into knots, just like middle school did.

But in two days we'd leave for Maine. Two months was a long time. Anything could happen.

Chapter 3

I jumped out of the car. Superior followed, barking, as I ran to the edge of the yard and looked at the bay, breathing in the cool sea air.

Our cottage sat high above the water on the east side of the Point. I glanced down the wooden stairs that led to our dock, then out at Bucket Island, then to the open waters of the ocean. My heart pounded, and my smile stretched so wide that it hurt.

We were only ninety miles from Boston, but I felt as if we were a million miles away.

"Lucy, I need your help!" Dad yelled.

"Well, Superior," I sighed, "you heard him. He needs us."

We ran to Dad and Bucky, who were unloading the car. Mr. and Mrs. Steele, our next-door neighbors, stood in the gravel by Dad.

"The Dorseys' cottage was perfectly fine and these new

owners have turned it into a . . ." Mr. Steele shook his cane at Dad. "Pierson Point will never be the same. It's the beginning of the end!"

I smiled. Mr. Steele liked to get all worked up about stuff. We'd been coming here every summer since I was born. Dad had been coming every summer since he was born, too. Things didn't change much. That was one of the things we loved about it.

Mr. Steele glanced down at me, his eyes softening. He and his wife had been here longer than any family on the Point. They had great stories about my grandparents and about Dad when he was little. But most important, they'd loved my mom. I hugged both of them.

"Goodness, Lucy, you've grown," Mrs. Steele said. "How was school?"

"Okay." I didn't want to talk about school. "Have you sold your kayak?"

During the off-season, everyone from the Point kept in touch through an email Listserv. I knew that Kiki Pollard had gotten into Bates College, the Grahams planned to build a new shed and the Steeles wanted to sell their three-year-old two-seat ocean kayak.

"Still for sale," Mrs. Steele said. "Hello, Superior. I see you've gotten grayer, like the rest of us. Your winter was good?"

Superior sat still, her eyes focused on me. Mrs. Steele didn't pet her. Everyone knew that when I was around, she paid attention only to me. That was her guide dog training.

"Superior, you're being rude. Answer Mrs. Steele." I giggled and she barked, swishing her tail. Her coat was black and shiny, although her paws and her snout were speckled with white. Was she whiter than the previous summer?

"Those new people put in a stone driveway," Mr. Steele said to Dad. "Can you imagine? *Here?*"

"Walter." Mrs. Steele sighed. "That's about enough."

The Dorsey Debacle—that was what Dad and I called the Dorseys' cottage. Twenty years earlier a huge oak tree had fallen on it, and the Dorsey cousins had fought so much over what to do about it that it had just sat empty. Five years ago a stockbroker from New York bought it, tore it down and built a two-story house with a garage, huge porch and balcony. Then he ran out of money and the house sat empty, weeds growing everywhere. It sold again a couple of months ago.

"Who bought it?" I asked.

"Someone from down your way," he said, scowling. "With a lot of money."

"We should be glad the place finally has someone to take care of it," Dad said. "It was a shame, sitting there."

"I'll tell you what's a shame. People building mansions, changing everything!"

I pinched my lips together, hiding my smile.

"Enough." Mrs. Steele winked at me. "Come see us and we'll catch up."

I nodded and they walked back to their cottage.

Dad stacked bags in the grass. "I've been coming here

forty-five years, through lots of changes. Can't imagine new Debacle owners will make a difference. No need to worry."

"I'm not worried." I picked up a duffel bag, then a second and swung them over my shoulders. Dad frowned, but I said, "They're not too heavy."

We moved up the walkway and pushed open the door. The porch was cool and smelled like mildew, but it was the best smell ever. My shoulders relaxed and warmth oozed into my arms. For two months it would be the four of us, doing what we did every summer. Dad would work on his book. Bucky would be with Henry Ramsey. And Superior and I would explore.

I flinched as I dropped the bags—they *were* too heavy—and hurried into the living room. My grandparents owned the cottage, but they didn't use it much anymore. Everything was as we had left it: Grandma's framed needlepoints on the walls, Granddad's clock on the mantel, the crocheted afghan on the couch. The torn wallpaper. The driftwood lamp. This room hadn't changed since Dad was a boy.

"It held up pretty well," Dad said. "Let's open it up."

Opening the cottage was a lot easier, and more fun, than closing it. Like most cottages on the Point, it was small, with a kitchen, living room, screened-in porch and half bathroom on the first floor. On the second there was a bigger bathroom, three tiny bedrooms and a large closet that Dad used as his writing room.

Dad turned on the water and put the screens in the windows while Bucky and I filled the refrigerator and cabinets with food. In my room I unpacked my clothes, my bird book, a sketch pad and art supplies for the day camp I was starting for the younger kids on the Point. Clay, paint, brushes, pads of paper and glue.

Dad said that Mom had always wanted to start a camp here. She'd called it a win-win for everyone: Moms got a break. Kids had fun.

I loved little kids and the idea of running a camp. All winter I had looked on the Web for things to do. The more plans I made—digging for crabs, building papier-mâché masks, painting rocks—the more excited I became.

I wanted the kids to have the *best* summer, one they'd never, ever forget.

"Lucy, I need help." Bucky's room was on the other side of Dad's, but the walls were so thin that I heard him.

"I know," I said to Superior, who stared at me from the rug. "I want to go outside, too." I walked down the hall, the knotted wooden floors creaking underneath me. I knew Dad would say, *Help him. He's only seven.*

I unzipped a bag of neatly folded clothes, packed by Jenny, and Bucky and I put them away. Toys were in the next bag. "You unpack this."

We went back to my room and Bucky plopped down on my bed, studying the framed pictures of Mom I'd brought from home. One was taken in front of her high school, where she was laughing with two other girls. In another she was older, sitting on the rocks at the end of the Point. The last was of the four of us, before she'd gotten sick.

18

"Which one do you think looks like her the most?" he asked.

I was six when Mom died, Bucky only one. I liked to be certain about Mom when we talked so he wouldn't be sad that he had no memories of her. "They all do."

"Who were these two girls?" He pointed to the picture. "Why are they laughing?"

We'd been over this a million times and I always had the same answer. "They were best friends and it was the first day of high school and they were happy because they found out that they had every class together. They wouldn't be alone."

"How do you know?" Bucky asked.

Dad didn't know who these girls were; we'd found the picture in a box after Mom had died. I didn't know how I knew the story. I just did.

"Bucky!" someone called from the lawn.

He ran to the window. "Henry!" Then he was out the door.

By the time Superior and I made it outside, Bucky and Henry were wrestling on the grass in front of the Ramseys', three cottages down. I'd promised Dad I'd make brownies for tonight's barbecue. Superior and I only had a few minutes to explore.

We ran. The east road followed our side of the Point, past the Steeles' and common property, before turning and connecting to the west road. The complete semicircle was a half mile. Twenty-five cottages were scattered along the roads.

At the common property I turned onto a path and walked through pine, birch and oak trees to the beach. Because of the rocks and grass, it wasn't much of a beach. At the far end huge boulders piled on top of each other into the water. Off to the left stood an abandoned lighthouse. I spun around, arms high. Nothing had changed.

I glanced up at the trees behind me. After the August storm the year before, Dad had borrowed the Ramseys' new kayak to check out the damage. Many trees had fallen, leaving an eagles' nest exposed. No one had ever seen an eagles' nest on the Point.

He'd come back excited. But when I had run down here, it had been high tide. The trees were too close to the water and I couldn't see up through the leaves to the nest.

It was low tide now. If I walked out far enough, I might have a better angle. I kicked off my flip-flops and stepped in. Icy water circled my ankles as Superior sat in the sand, watching.

Dad said that I'd liked to swim with Mom, but I rarely swam now. The water was too cold and you never knew what was underneath, hiding in the seaweed.

Superior wagged her tail. "Oh, you're fine now, but you don't like the water, either, you know." When the water was rough, she ran up and down the beach, barking at the waves. She was worse in the boat, hanging off the side, snapping at the wake. I glanced at my watch. The nest would have to wait. Time to go.

Back at the cottage I found the brownie mix and pulled out Grandma's old yellow mixing bowl. But I couldn't find the oil. I climbed the stairs, then stood in the doorway of Dad's writing room. He sat at his desk, staring at his computer.

"Ah, you caught me." He grinned. "I couldn't resist getting started again."

Dad was writing a book about Pierson Point. I had read a couple of chapter drafts. It was a lot easier to read than the other books he'd published, textbooks for his history classes back in Boston. It was way more interesting, too.

For example, in 1750 smugglers had supposedly buried stolen goods somewhere on the Point. In 1782 the Point had had more bald eagles' nests than any other place in Maine.

My favorite story was from Thaddeus Pierson's journal. He had lived on the Point in the early 1900s and his was the only personal account Dad had. Thaddeus had been a big outdoorsman. One day as he walked home, carrying a bucket of fish, a pack of wolves surprised him. He kept tossing the fish to the hungry wolves and just made it home.

I loved this story because I could see what the Point had been like back then.

But Dad said it might not be true; that was the problem with history. You weren't there, so you had to rely on other accounts, which were often unreliable.

"Think you'll finally be able to finish this summer?" I asked.

"I hope so." He raised his eyebrows. "Julia had an interesting idea."

"You let *her* read it?" What did she know? She'd never been here.

"No, but I was telling her about it."

"She's not a writer."

"True, but sometimes it's good to talk to someone who has a fresh perspective. They help you see things you didn't know are there."

He took off his glasses, chewed on the stem and turned his chair toward me. Dad had never been much of a talker. Until lately. Until the PT.

"I can't find the oil," I said.

"Goose." That was Dad's nickname for me.

"The barbecue starts soon!" I ran down the stairs and dug a bottle of walnut oil out of the cabinet. Wasn't that practically the same thing as vegetable oil? Jenny would know, but she was twelve hundred miles away. I could ask Mrs. Steele but she'd want to talk and I was saving that for later.

I didn't want Dad to think I couldn't do this. I poured in the oil, mixed the batter and put the pan in the oven.

Then I cleaned up. Our kitchen was small, with two windows, one held open with a yardstick. The wooden floor sloped down slightly, so the table wobbled unless you put a dish towel under one of the legs. The knob on the cabinet door was broken and you had to open it by putting your fingers into the grooves of the frame.

But I was home.

Chapter 4

The brownies looked great—thick, rich and oozing chocolate. I cut them into squares and put them on a paper plate.
But when I pulled off a corner and put it in my mouth, it
tasted awful. *Rancid,* as Jenny would say. I spit it into the sink.

Was it the walnut oil? I took the plate to the garbage.

"Ready?" Dad came into the kitchen. "Oh, can I taste?"

"They aren't—"

Just as he reached for a brownie, his phone rang. He
looked at the number and smiled. "Hi!"

The PT's face flashed into my mind—that enormous
mouth and those white teeth.

He turned away, then laughed. "I'll call you later. Me too."
When he reached for a brownie, still smiling, I yanked the
plate away.

"We won't have enough for tonight." What was I doing?
Nobody could eat these.

Dad shrugged, then hummed, something he didn't usually do. Neither of us carried our cell phones around up here, either. Now he fastened his onto his belt.

"Can't Superior come, just this once?" I asked.

"You know the rules. Superior and food don't mix."

Superior had only one fault. She begged for food, all the time. I scratched her under the chin and whispered, "We'll be back soon. Promise."

I followed Dad, the brownies in my hands. If I told him how awful they were, he'd want to know why I hadn't told him in the first place. Which I couldn't answer; it had happened so quickly.

We turned on the path next to the Grants' cottage and without looking at each other we took off running. Dad used to beat me easily, but the past summer I'd finally won. Now I turned at the oak tree and poured on the speed. I was first into the big field, the plate of brownies steady in my hands.

"Whew!" Dad bent over, breathing deeply. "I'm out of shape!"

We laughed and started across the field. Far off to the left were two old tennis courts, weeds sprouting through cracks along the baselines. A wooden play structure stood nearby. It was so old that it gave everyone splinters, but no one wanted to take it down.

We walked up to the Big House, a one-story meeting house with a wraparound porch. The families had built it in 1922 and it hadn't changed much. The floors creaked, the gutters leaked and it smelled like burned wood and mildew. We loved it. Mrs. Steele called it the heart of the Point, and I agreed.

I stopped in front of the steps. "These brownies aren't any good."

"Everything you make is great!" Dad smiled and disappeared into the Big House.

People were everywhere, walking through the field, crowding the porch. "How was your winter?" "How did your cottage hold up?" Hugs, kisses, slaps on backs.

I knew everyone, the Sullivans, the Tolls, the Averys, the Grants, the Pollards.

"We were so glad to get your email about camp," said Mrs. Dennis, holding her three-year-old, Stevie. "Lauren's excited! Stevie's too young, so maybe you could sit for us sometime?"

"Sure." I grinned at Stevie, who frowned and turned his face into his mom's neck.

"Lucy!" Mr. Ramsey was behind me. "Good to see you! Did you hear we've got new neighbors in the Dorsey house? From your neck of the woods."

I nodded. Lots of people from Boston vacationed or owned homes here. Someone grabbed Mr. Ramsey and said hello, so I slipped behind the crowd into the main room. Tables were stuffed with plates of food.

"Lucy!" Mrs. Ramsey hugged me. "Brownies! Your mom would've been proud! She always made the best ones. But I've told you that a hundred times."

"Yeah. But these are no good."

"So modest! Take them to the dessert table." She turned to talk to someone else.

No way.

In the kitchen, a new girl opened and shut drawers. She was maybe sixteen, with long blond hair streaked pink. She watched as I dumped the brownies into the trash. "Decided not to poison anyone?"

I laughed. "Exactly."

She had eyes so dark they were almost black and impossible to read. She smiled. "Are there any flashlights in this godforsaken place? My dad sent me in here for one."

I yanked on a drawer. It stuck, then screeched as I pulled harder. I reached in for a flashlight.

She raised her eyebrows. "I've asked three people and no one could help me."

"I know where everything is." I turned on the flashlight and nothing happened. I banged it on the counter and the light came on. "Sometimes you have to do that."

She took the flashlight. "You're like me. I always know what's going on."

"Well, not always," I said. But I stood taller. She wore a tank top, blue like the ocean, and jeans. Beaded earrings hung from her pierced ears. I touched my ears, which were still sore. Soon I'd wear earrings just like hers.

"Thanks, catch you later." She waved and disappeared into the main room.

You're like me. I smiled. No one had ever said that to me.

26

The main room was packed. Dad sat with the Steeles in the corner. Stevie cried as Mrs. Dennis pulled him out from under the dessert table. Kiki Pollard and the other older girls, Tonya and Danielle Winston, walked in.

I watched Kiki as she said hello to everyone. She was by far the nicest of the older girls. Before she drove into town, she would always ask neighbors if they needed anything. Two summers earlier she'd read every day to Mrs. Graham's mother, who had been ninety-two and recovering from eye surgery.

Right now she was bent over old Mr. Grant, talking, her hand on his shoulder.

Up here kids were either a lot older or a lot younger than me, so I was always alone with Superior—which I liked, because Superior was my best friend and so much fun.

Still, sometimes as I watched the older girls when we were at parties or while they went tubing in the bay, I liked to imagine that they'd ask me to hang out with them, a little-sister kind of thing. But they never paid much attention to me.

I sighed and walked outside. I looked up as Bucky limped toward me, blood trickling down his leg.

"I fell." He bit his lip, trying not to cry. I leaned closer. "Don't touch it!"

Bucky got hurt a lot because he was reckless. Falling off his bike, jamming his finger on a baseball. "It's not so bad. Let's go find a Band-Aid."

I got the first aid kit from the closet. The past winter, at my babysitting certification course at the YMCA, I'd learned

27

that you should wash a cut before putting on medicine and a bandage. But water would sting and Bucky might yell; people would think I couldn't take care of him. The cut wasn't bad. I smeared on ointment, then put on the bandage.

"Thanks, Lucy." He ran out the door, past a woman I'd never seen before.

Mrs. Ramsey pointed to her and said, "Will you go see what she brought?"

I walked up to the woman. She had long, perfect brown hair and wore a blue skirt and a stiff white shirt. Something about how tall she stood, head forward, mouth open, made me think she was so hungry she could eat everything in the room.

"Hi," I said. "Nice pie. I can take that for you."

She had rain clouds in her eyes. No—her eyes weren't cloudy, but gray-green. She broke into a gigantic smile.

"Aren't you nice!" Her voice was high and excited as she handed me the pie. Then her smile faded. "I had to hold it all the way from Boston. Does it look okay?"

"It looks great!"

"Whew!" The pie had perfectly pinched edges. She probably knew all those mom things, what to do with walnut oil, where to shop for the right kind of underwear and how to make sure your newly pierced ears didn't get infected.

"What's your name?" she asked.

"Lucy Gallagher. We live on the east road."

"I know you! We're neighbors back home. You go to school with my son."

My gaze followed her outstretched arm to the porch. Ian

28

Richards stood on the steps, staring at the field, his hands jammed in the front pockets of his jeans.

"We just moved in today," she said. "Such a wonderful spot. We bought the Dorsey house on the west road. Ian! Come say hello to Lucy."

Ian? On porch. Bought Dorsey house. On *my* Pierson Point. Was this a joke?

Ian's wild blond hair was combed off his forehead and he wore a bright purple polo shirt. He raised his eyebrows at me and didn't move.

I felt my blood throb in my cheeks.

Mrs. Richards sighed. "I understand there aren't many boys up here."

No. No way will I hang out with Ian. Wait until I tell Mei!

Mrs. Richards seemed so nice. How could she be Ian's mom? And *how* had they found this place?

Mrs. Ramsey walked up, took the pie and led Mrs. Richards away.

"Lucy!" Bucky yelled. I walked down the porch steps, past Ian and onto the grass. Becca, Olivia and Bucky pushed Henry on the rope swing that hung from a tree next to the Big House.

"Wanna play chase?" Becca called. She and Olivia would both be in my camp the next week.

"After dinner." Chase was a game I'd made up the year before, a combination of hide-and-seek and kick the can. Ian walked down the steps and stood near me.

"Oh," Becca whined. "Can't we play now?"

"No, later, I promise," I said. Henry leaped off the swing and they ran away.

I glanced at Ian, my heart pounding, my face hot. He looked at me, then dropped his eyes.

"Who *told* you about this place?" I asked.

Ian shrugged. "My dad grew up in Maine."

"Did you know that I live up here?"

"Yeah, the Realtor dude told us."

"Well, why didn't you say something to me?"

"What's the big deal?" He kicked the grass.

I clenched my hands. "Just so you know, people here don't bug each other."

"Okay."

"Nobody shows off or teases each other. Families have been coming here for generations and hardly anyone fights with each other. You better remember that."

"I'm new, so you think you can boss me around?"

"I'm not bossing you around."

"Yeah, you are, Bossy Boss. Jeez, nice welcome party."

I glared at him. Then the girl with pink streaks walked around the Big House and he said, "Allison, Mom's looking for you inside."

"Tell her I'm going back. This party is so lame." She tossed her pink-streaked hair behind her, then walked across the field. Ian started up the steps.

In my head I heard Mr. Steele: *Pierson Point will never be the same.*

Chapter 5

The next morning I woke, my sore ear throbbing against the pillow. I rolled onto my back, and the pain disappeared. Then I watched a spider make its way across my wall. Maybe it'd be my friend, like Charlotte was to Wilbur. A new friend here on the Point.

Ian. I pulled my quilt up to my neck.

For our science project the past winter, we had studied water sources. Our teacher put us in pairs, then assigned each pair a country. Ian and I got Egypt. Everyone had to research, write a PowerPoint presentation and give it to the class.

When we went to the library to do research, all the computers were taken, so Mrs. Jonas let Ian use hers. I went to find books. When I came back, everyone was working, except Ian, who was staring at a blank screen.

I had the instructions that our teacher had given us the day before. I sighed, "No wonder you don't know what to do!"

As I said this, the room grew quiet. Everyone looked at us. Someone snickered.

Ian laughed, too, then gave me a dirty look. "You think I'm *stupid*, Miss Brainiac?"

That wasn't what I'd meant. "Ian, I . . ."

"Shut up," he hissed. "I can do this myself."

I sat, face burning, and opened a book about water shortages.

"What are you doing?" Mrs. Jonas stood over us, her hands on her hips.

"Lucy pulled it up," Ian said. On the computer a man ran across a stage, then mooned the audience, his naked bottom bright white.

Mrs. Jonas gasped and closed her laptop. "On my computer!"

"I didn't do that!" I said.

"Yes, you did, Lucy Goosey." Ian's voice was loud.

Several boys laughed. My friends, near the door, stood up to watch.

"No, I didn't!" How could he be so mean, such a liar?

Mrs. Jonas took us to her office and shut the door. She frowned at me.

"I didn't do it," I said.

Mrs. Jonas looked at Ian.

"Why blame me?" he said, crossing his arms. "Because Lucy's a perfect student?"

"I am not!" I said.

"Stop, both of you!" she said. "Ian, what happened?"

We glared at each other. Then he uncrossed his arms and grinned. "I was just trying to have a little fun."

Mrs. Jonas sighed. "Lucy, go back to work. Ian, I'd like to have a word with you."

In the library I sat down and stared at my book. Ian didn't come back.

We got an A, although I did most of the project. But I'm not a perfect student. I have to work hard. Did *that* make me bossy? Or a brainiac?

Now I swung my legs over the side of my bed. With my toes I scratched Superior's neck. Cool air blew through my window, sending goose bumps up my arms.

Maine had plenty of peninsulas and islands. Why did Ian have to come to this one?

I jumped out of bed and grabbed my notebook and bird book. After Superior ate and I had breakfast, we started down the road. On the path to the water, the air was cool and smelled like dirt and pine. Down at the beach the sky was so clear that I saw Pear Island and, farther out, Upper Egg Island.

I walked to the farthest rock and ran my fingers over the dozens of snails attached to the boulders. Mom and I liked how bumpy and smooth they felt and we were careful not to pull them off.

This was where I wanted to be, near the water—smelling it, hearing it. That day it was perfect, sparkling blue and silver, waves gentle.

I sat and flipped through *Birds of America*. Mrs. Jonas had given it to me on our last day of school. "Here, Lucy," she'd said. "Since you're the only student in the last forty years to check it out of the library, you might as well take it with you."

"Really?" I'd laughed. "Forty years? Thanks!"

I knew the torn and yellowed pages by heart, the wild turkey and Bachman's warbler. The white-headed eagle took up two pages. I closed the book and picked up my notebook. It was filled with drawings of things at the Point and every year I added to it.

Right now I wanted to draw an eagle, from memory. My art teacher could do this. But when I tried to go inside, as she called it, the idea got lost. If I had something to see, to copy, I could draw it.

Superior startled and I looked up to see a pair of seagulls circle above us. I looked down at my blank page and sighed. No use.

I opened my bird book to the eagles. The male and female stood next to each other, eyes slanted in confident stares. Eagles didn't travel in flocks but mated for life. They were partners, even taking turns sitting on their eggs. They built nests in sturdy nooks near the treetops, in the open, because nothing preyed on them. And every year they came back to the same nests and made them bigger, stronger.

I'd never seen Dad as excited as he was the day he found the nest. I was in my room when he charged up the stairs. "You have to see it, Goose, it's amazing!"

"Can we take the boat?" Then I could sit on a seat next to Dad, holding on.

"Too rocky for the speedboat. You'll have to take the Ramseys' kayak."

I nodded but didn't move. I'd never been in a kayak.

One night when the PT came to dinner and Dad told her about the amazing nest, I came up with an idea. I'd use the money I'd make from camp to buy Dad his own kayak for his birthday. Then he could see the eagles whenever he wanted.

I looked up to see a fishing boat, the only boat moving this early. Later the bay would fill with boats, kayaks, tubes.

And Ian.

But the Point was so big that you could go weeks without seeing everyone. If I ignored him, he wouldn't be able to twist my words around or tease me.

My stomach started grumbling and we headed back. We stopped at the Steeles' cottage and looked in through the screen. Mrs. and Mr. Steele were at the kitchen table.

"Come in!" Mrs. Steele pulled out a chair. She poured a glass of orange juice for me and a bowl of water for Superior. "Goodness, you look more and more like your mom!"

"Thanks!" Mrs. Steele said this every summer.

"I saw on the email exchange that you're starting a camp," she said.

"Every Monday and Wednesday morning."

"That's a lot to take on!" Mrs. Steele said. "Your mom was so good with kids. Remember, Walt, how she'd take the little ones after parties and play hide-and-seek?"

"She was good at everything!" Mr. Steele grunted. "Kind, too."

Everyone had liked my mom.

Mrs. Steele brought a plate of muffins to the table. I took one, still warm and plump with blueberries. It was so delicious that I nearly finished it in three bites, but I slipped the last piece under the table to Superior. Her tongue was warm against my palm.

"Heard you know the Dorsey owners," Mrs. Steele said. "Tell us about them."

"Ian's my age, Allison's older. I didn't meet their dad but their mom is nice."

"I met him. Owns a business," Mr. Steele said. "A real go-getter!"

"It'll be nice for you to have a friend up here," Mrs. Steele said.

"Yeah." Allison was older, but she *could* be my friend.

"You should show him around," she said. "There's so much to see."

Ian? I drained my juice. "How was your winter?"

"Not cold enough! Global warming." Mr. Steele grunted.

Under the table Superior stretched across my feet, her body warm and heavy. I reached down to stroke her head and she licked my hand.

"Talked to your grandma yesterday. She sends her love," Mrs. Steele said. "Too bad they won't be up this summer."

I nodded. My grandparents usually came up for a week or two, but they had decided to spend that summer in Colorado with Granddad's brother, who'd just had surgery.

36

"Walt, remember how Lucy's mom used to make her granddad laugh?"

He grunted again.

"She made *all* of us laugh. Such an open, free spirit." She told me this every summer but I couldn't picture what she meant. When I asked Jenny about it, she said to imagine Mom standing in the open and letting the wind take her.

I got up to go and Mrs. Steele pushed the plate toward me. I took another muffin and said, "Thanks!" as I bounced out the door.

Outside, the wind blew through my hair and swirled dried-up leaves at my feet. On windy days I sometimes stood on the rocks at the beach and held out my arms, trying to let the wind take me. But all I ever felt were tangles in my hair and ocean spray on my skin.

Inside our cottage I listened to the quiet. Back in Boston, we'd moved into our house only months before Mom got sick, so I wasn't sure what had been there before she died, or what came after. But up here I *remembered* her.

Working on puzzles. Stretched across the bed, pillow bunched under her chin. Standing at the living room window in her flowered sundress. We'd held hands as we had explored the shore under the dock, and we'd eaten cereal in the mornings, side by side, at the wobbly table in the kitchen.

Dad told me that the first time he brought Mom here, she ran to the water and burst into tears. It reminded her of where she'd grown up, on Lake Superior in Michigan's Upper Peninsula, only she loved here much better.

I heard Dad's voice and climbed the stairs. Usually he didn't talk while working. He sat, phone to his ear, and motioned me into his room. I stayed in the hall.

"Thanks, I'll call later." He smiled as he hung up. "That was Julia."

Ignore her. That's the best way to make something go away. "How's it going?"

"Big news! Someone from the historical society found a journal, dating from the early nineteen hundreds. The writer lived on the Point."

"And it's real?"

"Yep. One of the old houses in town sold last spring and the new owners found it tucked into a hole in the foundation. This throws my project into *complete* disarray." But he smiled.

"Isn't that bad?"

"No, it's another source. Wonder how it'll hold up next to Thaddeus's."

"Why do you need another source? Isn't Thaddeus's enough?"

"History's a funny thing, Goose. Two people can see the same event, yet tell it differently. Thaddeus and the journal writer lived here around the same time. Could be very telling how they both talk about things."

How could you ever be sure that anything in history was true?

Dad stood, fastening his phone to his belt. "I'm headed into town to take a look at this. Bucky's in his room. Will you stay with him until I get back? I won't be long."

"Sure." I sat at his desk. Dad had been on the computer nonstop, so now was my first chance to go on email. Rachel and Annie were at sleepaway camp with no computers, but Mei wasn't going to her camp until the second half of summer. I told her about Ian and ended with *When are you going to come up here? And what am I going to do about Ian? Help!*

I glanced out the window and saw Mrs. Richards walking by. I leaned on the sill. She looked as if she'd walked out of a magazine, with her green skirt and blouse and perfect hair. I leaned out farther. Maybe she'd call to me, ask more questions.

But Ian followed. As they got closer I saw that Mrs. Richards was frowning and staring at the road. Why didn't Ian catch up? Maybe he'd done something wrong.

Then Ian looked up at me and I dove to the floor. It wouldn't be easy avoiding him after all.

Chapter 6

At nine a.m. I stood next to the Big House, holding my clipboard with the morning's plan, Superior at my feet. "Camp's open!" I shouted.

The six-year-olds, Olivia and Lauren, sat near me. Becca, who was nine, ran toward me with Bucky and the eight-year-olds: her brother, Peter, and Henry.

"We'll start with playing chase, then do a craft."

"Yay! Chase!" Becca yelled.

"Craft? When do we play baseball?" Peter pointed to his glove on the steps.

Baseball? But we didn't have enough equipment. "How about kickball on Wednesday?"

"Okay."

We played chase until Lauren started to cry. "I'm not playing. I'm always the first one caught."

I sat next to her. Her brown hair fluttered in the breeze

and she had a big space where her two front teeth should be. When I was six, I didn't have front teeth, either. I leaned over and whispered, "How about we *always* be teammates?"

She nodded and wiped her tears on her stuffed polar bear. Then she helped me bring out pretzel bags and juice boxes for everyone.

I squatted and scratched Superior behind her ears. The Point was quiet. Parents who commuted from Portland and Boston had gone back to work. No sign of Ian. And even though we were off schedule, camp was going okay.

"Can we have more juice?" Peter asked. I tossed a box and he caught it in his baseball glove. Everyone laughed. The woman who taught the babysitting course said kids should drink lots of fluids. Good thing I had bought so many drinks. They were all tired, their faces red and sweaty, but they seemed happy.

Little kids were great, because they just wanted to have fun. One day the past summer when I'd babysat for Lauren, we'd played with a balloon for two hours, trying to keep it in the air. And little kids could play with anyone. They didn't care if you were different.

Craft time. I went inside for glue and Popsicle sticks. When I returned, Ian walked across the field toward us, lacrosse stick in his hand. The boys stopped talking.

"What are you doing?" Ian asked.

"It's camp," Lauren said. "Lucy's camp."

"*Camp?*" Ian said. "You have a *camp*? Oh! Can I join?"

Peter giggled. Everyone looked at Ian, then at me.

Ian wore gym shorts to his knees and a T-shirt. His cowlick stood up like a cresting wave and he squinted as he smirked. "How do you know how to run a camp?"

"It's like babysitting." He followed as I walked around, picking up juice boxes.

"Yeah, but who said you could do this?" he asked.

"I just decided."

"How do you know what to do?"

Everyone was quiet, watching. "I just do."

Peter walked over to Ian. "Is your lacrosse stick new?"

"Yeah," Ian said. Peter just kept staring at him.

It was almost noon and we hadn't started the craft. Only Lauren and Olivia wanted to do it, so I showed them how to glue Popsicle sticks in a square, making a frame. Bucky and Henry set up army men. When Ian squatted in front of Superior, Peter squatted, too.

I walked to Superior and patted her head. She leaned into my leg.

"Great dog." Ian smiled at her but didn't try to pet her. "What's her name?"

"Superior," I said. She looked up at me. Smart girl. Don't trust him! I thought.

He stood. "Our next-door neighbor told me that pirates buried treasure here years ago. And your dad's writing a book about the Point."

"Supposedly smugglers buried stolen goods somewhere on

the Point. But my dad doesn't think it's true. He never said anything about pirates."

"Smugglers, pirates, same thing."

"No, they aren't."

"Sure they are."

"I don't think so."

"What's the difference?"

Was there a difference? Then Ian grinned. He was trying to tangle me up.

"Ian, wanna push me on the swing?" Peter asked.

"Okay."

Peter jumped onto the small plastic saucer that was tied to the end of the rope. Ian pushed, and Peter tipped back his head, laughing, as he flew through the air in big looping circles.

"That's enough," Peter yelled. Ian let the swing slow down as the girls and I started putting the art supplies back in the box.

Bucky yelled, "Don't do that!"

Holding the rope above Peter, Ian jumped onto the back of the saucer. The tree branch groaned as they sailed out into the yard. Then the rope snapped and they fell hard onto the ground. We ran to them.

Peter rolled onto his stomach, his face buried in his elbows. I leaned over him, my hand on his back. "Peter?" *Please let him be okay*, I thought.

He turned over and wiped his face on his shirt, leaving

streaks of dirt and tears. He rubbed his shoulder but seemed okay.

Whew! I sat back. The rope had snapped near the top and now only a small part hung from the branch. The rest sprawled across the grass. I glared at Ian.

"Sorry," Ian said.

Peter smiled slightly. "It's all right."

"The rule is only one person on the swing at a time," Becca said.

"Well, I didn't know about any rule," Ian said.

Learning to swing on the rope was a rite of passage, Dad said. I was four when Mom taught me. You placed hand over hand above you. And the secret to hanging on was crossing your legs over the rope and squeezing.

"Lucy, you can fix it, right?" Lauren's lower lip trembled.

"Oh, my dad'll fix it," Ian said. "Or put up a new one. This one looks pretty old."

"It was *fine*." How could he act as if this were no big deal? I stomped up the stairs with the art supplies.

When I came back, Ian was gone. Peter and Becca ran to the tennis courts to meet their mom. Bucky and I walked the others home.

Along the way they fired questions at me. Why had he jumped on the swing? How would we fix the rope? Who would pay for it? Was Ian in big trouble?

I didn't know how to answer. Was I responsible, since it happened during camp? I started walking faster, hands clenched.

44

After we dropped everyone off, Bucky and I walked back to the cottage.

"I don't like Ian," Bucky said as he opened our porch door.

"Me neither."

Dad stood at the stove in his old flannel shirt, making grilled cheese sandwiches. "Hey, how'd it go?"

"Ian broke the rope swing!" Bucky said, then told him what had happened.

Dad peeled back the bread tops and scattered Goldfish crackers on the melting cheese, as Mom used to do. "I'm just glad Peter's okay."

"But, Dad, Ian *broke* it," I said. "Won't everyone be mad?"

"Oh, I don't know. A couple of us were talking about the swing at the barbecue. It was old, an accident waiting to happen. It's time for a new one."

Bucky and I exchanged frowns.

Dad put the sandwiches on plates and we headed to the dock. After I ate, I stretched out on my stomach, the warm wood heating me. Bucky crouched, looking through the slats. Superior sat at attention, staring at the water.

"Look, the seals!" Dad pointed.

Past the moored boats I saw the black shiny heads of a dozen seals sunning themselves on rocks.

"Tell the story about when Mom saw the seals for the first time," Bucky said.

Dad laughed. "She didn't know what they were. Came running up to the cottage, yelling, 'The rocks are moving. The rocks are moving!'" Bucky giggled.

45

I smiled. "They didn't have wild seals in Michigan."

Dad nodded, grinning. "They sure didn't."

I remembered Mom here on the dock, wind blowing her hair as she shaded her eyes with her hand and looked out at the water.

"Can we go to Pear today?" Bucky asked.

"I need to work," Dad said. "I brought back the new journal. The author turned out to be Walter Steele's grandma Edna Monahan. She lived here at the same time as Thaddeus. Imagine that, a hundred years ago!"

Before most of the cottages had been built—and the Big House, tennis courts and rope swing, too. I brought my knees to my chest. Ian didn't care one bit about breaking the swing.

Dad nudged my shoulder. "I'm sure camp was great. The kids probably loved it."

I nodded. Would Ian show up on Wednesday?

"Don't worry about the swing, Goose. It sounds like it was an accident. I'll go with you later to tell Joel Ramsey about it. Okay?"

"Okay," I said. Mr. Ramsey was president of the Point that summer.

Dad cleared his throat. "There's something I want to talk to you about."

Bucky had been leaning over the dock, his arm in the water, but now he sat up. I hugged my knees tighter. I didn't like how serious his voice sounded.

"Julia's coming to Portland in two weeks, staying for the

weekend with friends, and so I thought we could invite her up that Sunday."

"But what would we do with her all day?" I asked.

"What we always do. Picnics. Walks."

"Can we take her camping on Upper Egg?" Bucky asked.

I shot him a look. The past year we'd taken a friend of Dad's hiking at Pear, but we'd never taken *anyone* camping. "But she won't know anyone."

"She's pretty friendly," Dad said. "I think it'll be okay."

The art historian Dad had dated a couple of years earlier had never come here to visit and she hadn't come to our house in Boston much. The PT had been around a lot. The first time I met her, she tripped and fell over our coatrack.

Aside from being a klutz, she smiled too much. She had this huge mouth with teeth the size of piano keys. Her smile was blinding.

"Lucy?" Dad's smile faded and I felt a sting in my chest.

"I don't care."

"Can we go to Pete's for ice cream, huh, Dad?" Bucky asked.

I felt Dad staring at me, but I didn't look up. He said, "After dinner."

"Can't we go now?"

"Buck." Dad frowned. "I've got to work."

Bucky huffed extra loudly and I shook my head at him. Dad didn't get angry at us very often, but I couldn't stand it when he did. Like last year when Bucky put a hole through our couch with a screwdriver, Dad was *so* mad. He wouldn't talk for the whole day and I felt awful, even though it wasn't my fault.

I just liked it best when Dad was happy.

He started up the stairs. I stared at the water. *Great.*

Chapter 7

On Thursday morning Lauren and I stood inside her cottage, waving good-bye to Mrs. Dennis and Stevie. My first babysitting job of the summer, not counting camp. I looked at the knotty paneling and bookcases. It was like our cottage, only it didn't smell like mildew.

Lauren circled me, following Superior. Finally Superior wiggled between my legs and looked up: *Help!* Lauren sighed, her shoulders falling.

"I'm sorry," I said. "Superior's a little different, remember? She's friendly, but most of the time she doesn't let anyone but me pet her."

Lauren sat, her polar bear, Poley, in her lap and tears in her eyes. I couldn't stand that she was sad, so I sat next to her. Superior stayed close, but just out of Lauren's reach.

"She was trained to listen to one person," I said. "I'm that person now."

"You're like her mom," Lauren said.

I'd never thought of it like that. I pulled a dog treat from my pocket and handed it to Lauren. She put it in her palm and when Superior took it, she quickly petted her.

She grinned and jumped up. "Let's go see the neighbors' new dock."

The air was cool and damp and the sky was gray. I turned the corner into the backyard and stared at a huge new dock at Ian's house, the Debacle. It took up the entire waterfront with its wooden beams, shiny metal posts and boathouse.

"Let's see if the jellyfish came back, the ones that don't sting." Lauren ran to the water and waded in.

I glanced back at the Debacle. Dozens of windows stretched across the house. Bushes and flowers lined the deck. Allison waved from a chair, then walked toward us.

"Like the new dock?" She wore big dangling earrings and carried a book.

"What was wrong with the old one?" I asked. Lauren walked up next to me.

"Probably nothing. My dad's a builder, so he builds things. *Big*, new things."

"What's that?" Lauren pointed to Allison's book.

"Drawings." She opened her notebook. Inside were pencil drawings of buildings, bridges and statues. Her lines were straight, the details sharp. On one building you could see every brick, every skinny layer of mortar. These drawings must have taken her hours.

"They're really good." I pointed to a building. "Think your dad could build that?"

She shrugged. "Yeah, right. He's never sat still long enough to look at them."

"Oh." I paused. "Did you copy them from a book?"

"No. I made them up."

"Wow. I like to draw, too."

She raised her eyebrows. "Another thing we have in common."

I grinned, then shook my head. "Oh, no, I'm not near as good as you."

"Hello, there!" Mrs. Richards called as she walked over. Her long hair was in a ponytail and she wore a short pink skirt and sandals with sparkles.

"Hi!"

She smiled at me, then turned to Allison. "Did you ask Lucy about the trash?"

Allison looked at me. "Last night we put the trash in the garbage can and this morning it was all over the yard. *I* had to pick it up."

"Oh, raccoons probably got into it. You should either keep your trash inside your garage with the door closed or tie it in bags and put it on top of your car. Then you can take it to the Dumpsters. Trash pickup is every Tuesday."

"Aha!" Mrs. Richards nodded. "I kept seeing trash bags on cars."

Allison snorted. "You put *trash* on your *car*? What are they, super raccoons?"

"They're nocturnal," Mrs. Richards said.

Allison rolled her eyes. "I know they're nocturnal."

51

"What's nocturnal?" Lauren asked.

"It means they sleep during the day and come out at night," Allison said. "And they're omnivorous, so they eat plants, animals, anything. Their scientific name is *Procyon lotor*. Native Americans called them *aroughcun*, which translates, 'he who scratches with his hands.'"

Wow! She was an encyclopedia.

"You sure know a lot about raccoons," Lauren said.

"Just one of those stupid things you learn in school."

"Do you have a photographic memory?" I asked.

"Something like that," Allison said. Mrs. Richards sighed. Allison grinned at me.

"Well, I'd love to hear more pointers, Lucy." Mrs. Richards turned for her house. "How about stopping by soon for a glass of iced tea?"

"Okay." My smile got bigger and bigger as I watched her go into the house.

When I turned back, Allison was staring at me. "My mom said you're in class with Ian. Poor you."

I hesitated.

"Don't tell me he has you fooled, too. Mr. Personality! I thought at least *you'd* see through him."

I *did* see through him! But it didn't feel right to bad-mouth him to his sister.

I hadn't seen Ian since he'd broken the swing. Mr. Ramsey told me that Ian had apologized. Had he gotten in trouble? Was that why I hadn't seen him?

We turned as a speedboat approached. Kiki, her red hair blowing behind her, pulled up to the dock. Tonya jumped out, rope in hand, and tied the boat. They waved.

"Where's your new inner tube?" Kiki yelled.

"I'll get it!" Allison waved back.

"Come on, before the rain!" Tonya said.

"Later, kiddos." Allison stuck her book on the deck, reached underneath and rolled a giant inner tube down to the dock.

Tonya helped Allison put it in the boat. They jumped on board and Kiki waved as she drove away.

I smiled as they grew smaller and smaller under the gray sky. So, Allison was friends with the older girls. And I was friends with Allison.

For lunch we went into town, to the Clam Shack. We ordered clams, root beers, french fries and onion rings and took everything outside to a picnic table.

The rain was soft and misty and fell silently on the umbrella above us. This was our favorite place to eat, and because of the weather, we had it to ourselves.

Dad's phone rang. "It's Grandma."

He set his phone on the table and pressed Speaker. Bucky and I said hello.

"Hello, you two. How are the clams? How is the Point?"

"Everything's great," I said. "But it'll be weird without you up here."

That was true, although it might be more relaxing. Grandma had the energy of five people, Dad always said.

"We'll miss you, too, sweetie. Oh! My *goodness!*"

"What?"

"Granddad and I are at a restaurant," she whispered. "And this man just walked by. Strangest thing. One of his eyes didn't move or blink. It must be a glass eye."

"How do you get a glass eye?" Bucky asked.

"Don't know. Think of the fun! You could take it out and play marbles with it."

Bucky laughed. "You could play catch with it."

This had to be one of Grandma's crazy stories. We knew she made them up, but I went along. "At night you could leave it on your nightstand and it could watch you sleep." We laughed, even Dad.

"How's Uncle Bud?" Dad asked.

"The surgery went fine but the recovery's been tough."

Dad shook his head. "He was always so strong."

"It's just life, Ben," Grandma said. "He's going to be okay for now, so no sad business, okay?"

Dad glanced at me.

"Well, I need to go," Grandma said. "Big kisses to you all."

We said good-bye and finished our lunch. Then we were back in the car. When Dad turned onto the dirt road to the Point, I opened the window. The smell of pine and cool sea air filled the car.

No sad business. Grandma was talking about how sad we'd

been, especially Dad, after Mom had died. He kept crying and barely left his room. It scared me so much that I tried not to think about it.

I twisted my earrings and looked out the window.

The mist had turned to light rain and the wipers squeaked across the windshield. Patches of fog hung in the trees between the Averys' and Pollards' cottages.

Superior waited for us at the porch door. Later she lay across my feet while I sat in front of the puzzle on the table.

I liked puzzles because even if they seemed impossible, eventually you'd put them together. Every summer I did one, and this was the hardest yet, two thousand tiny pieces of an ocean scene.

Dad sat next to me and picked up a blue piece. He hummed, studying it. Dad wasn't sad very often. I wasn't, either, although sometimes when I thought about Mom—not the fun stuff we usually talked about—I felt something heavy start to fill up this big space inside me. Was it sadness? Maybe it was just that I missed her.

I went back to the puzzle. I had a system. I separated the pieces with edges and tried to make the border. Then I separated the other pieces into colors. After that I just went for it.

Dad still held the same blue piece. He stared at the edges, then the puzzle, then back. But he was studying so hard that he missed the obvious.

"*Dad.*" I took his piece and fit it into the ocean. "It was right in front of you!"

"I'm no good at this. I didn't see it." We laughed. "Let's go down to the dock."

We walked across the yard and down the stairs. The dock was cool and damp under my bare feet. We got onto our stomachs and looked through the slats. On sunny days it was easy to see, but that day the water was murky and dark.

"I see . . . well, not much," Dad said.

We'd played this game ever since I could remember, trying to see who could find the most unusual thing. One time Dad found a wallet with fifty dollars on the sand.

"I see minnows, starboard side," I said.

"What? Are you making that up?"

"Sore loser!" I laughed, then rolled over and sat. Fog drifted over the water, hiding the buoys and boats in a soft white haze.

"Oh, I forgot to tell you," Dad said. "Ian and his dad came by while you were babysitting. He seems like a nice kid. Polite."

"Ian's not polite."

"He was today. And quiet. His dad talks a lot. Big guy. Said he's taking the summer off to work on the house. Landscaped, put in a new dock."

"Did his dad say anything about the rope swing?" I asked.

"No. But he thought the Big House might have some water damage."

"What do you mean?"

"He pulled back some shingles and found rotten wood. Can't say I'm surprised."

"What's going to happen?"

"Maybe just repairs, although he said we should think about tearing it down. He'd help with something new, bigger. He had lots of ideas." Dad grinned.

"Tear it down!" I said. "Really?"

"Whoa, nobody wants anything to happen to the Big House. Let's just wait and see what he finds when he takes a closer look."

I sank. The Big House had been here for almost a hundred years. Everyone on the Point had some kind of memory about it. Mom had loved the Big House. We couldn't tear it down.

Chapter 8

$\mathcal{I}$ took my shoe box from under my bed and counted my money: one hundred dollars in twenties, tens and singles. I'd have had a lot more if I hadn't spent so much on snacks and craft supplies.

From under the money I pulled out the boat magazine and opened to the kayak I'd circled. Durable polyethylene hull, adjustable padded backrest, lightweight at only forty pounds. It came with a storage cover and a carbon fiber paddle and I'd need every dollar from camp and babysitting to pay for it.

"Lucy, time to go," Dad called.

I glanced at the other kayaks, cheaper but not as nice. Then I put back the magazine, shoved the box under my bed and ran down the stairs.

Dad and Bucky were outside next to my wagon, which was filled with supplies for the night. We were on our way to the July Fourth clambake at the beach. I stood inside on the porch with Superior. "If we could trust you, you'd be invited."

Three years earlier she'd stolen a hot dog out of Mrs. Pollard's hand, and ever since, she'd been banned whenever food was served. She pulled back her ears. I hugged her.

"Don't worry," I said. "I promise to be back before the fireworks."

At the beach I spread our blanket next to the Steeles'. Then I set our plates and silverware on the blanket. I breathed in the thick smell of burning charcoal and wood.

"Lucy!" Becca ran up. "We need you! For chase!"

"After dinner," I said. Then Henry called her and she took off.

The older girls sat on the rocks. I walked down to the water, closer to them. Kiki, wearing a Bates sweatshirt, said something that made everyone laugh but I was too far away to hear. I should just walk up to them and say hi.

But I'd tried that at a party the summer before. They'd stared at me as I'd walked up and stood there and then Kiki had asked, "Do you want something, Lucy?"

She asked nicely. But I felt like an idiot, because suddenly I didn't know *what* I wanted. And so I said the first thing that came to mind. "The blues aren't biting yet."

Kiki bunched up her eyebrows, confused. "The bluefish? What?"

Tonya giggled. My face burned as I ran off.

Maybe if someone went with me, I'd feel braver. Too bad Mei hadn't come to visit yet.

Allison, sitting next to Kiki, smiled at me. But as I started toward them, she turned away.

I looked around. Mrs. Richards stood alone at the water, barely blinking her rain-cloud eyes as she looked out into the bay.

"Lucy!" Lauren ran up. I pretended to run away in slow motion. She grabbed my legs and we fell, giggling.

Mrs. Richards stood over us, smiling. "You goofballs."

"Dinner's ready!" Mrs. Graham yelled.

"Lucy." Henry ran up to me. "We wanna play chase."

"After dinner," I said.

Henry groaned. "It's gonna get dark!"

"Want to see what I found?" Lauren pulled on my hand.

"Goodness." Mrs. Richards laughed. "It must feel good to be needed so much."

I blushed. "Well, I made up this game and everyone wants me to play because they get confused about the rules."

"Could you ask Ian to join?" Mrs. Richards asked.

I squeezed my hand into a fist. Ian wouldn't want to play with the younger kids.

Mrs. Richards sighed. "He's having a hard time."

"Oh." *Ian?*

A man walked up and Mrs. Richards said, "This is my husband, John."

"Hello!" Mr. Richards had dark eyes, like Allison and Ian, and a deep, booming voice. With his white hair and wrinkles at the corners of his eyes, he seemed a lot older than Mrs. Richards. We shook, his huge hand practically swallowing mine.

"This is Lucy, Ian's friend from home," Mrs. Richards said.

Mr. Richards nodded. "Oh, sure, sure, met your dad and brother."

I pulled my hand away and stood taller. "Hi."

"I hear this clambake has been a tradition for years," he said. "Wonderful idea."

I nodded. "We have *lots* of traditions. The talent show. The fishing contest. The regatta. See Mr. and Mrs. Steele over there? They've been coming to the Point since, like, the 1950s. Everybody pretty much likes things to stay just the way they are."

Mr. Richards's eyes flitted to something over my shoulder. Had he heard me?

"You can tell us about these traditions when you stop by." Mrs. Richards smiled.

"I will!"

"Oh, there's Brad Avery," Mr. Richards said.

He nudged Mrs. Richards and she winked as they walked off. I joined Dad and Bucky in the food line; then we sat on our blanket. I watched Mr. Richards talking to everyone. He seemed okay.

Mrs. Richards and Ian sat on their blanket, eating. I couldn't ask him to play chase, because I didn't trust him.

Lauren yelled, "Lucy! Time to play!"

What to do about Ian? I didn't want Mrs. Richards to be mad at me.

"Lucy!" Becca called.

"I'm coming." I jumped up and started walking. Ian would probably break something else. Tease me. Scare the kids. I kept going until I stood in front of him. "Wanna go to the field to play a game?"

Mrs. Richards lit up. "You should go."

Ian poked the sand with a stick. Was he even listening? But when I started to walk away, he followed.

The sun had gone down behind the trees but the sky was still light. The air smelled like smoke, clams and salt water, then like dirt and pine as we went down the path. It was quiet, the voices from the beach fading, our steps cushioned by pine needles.

I glanced back at him. He'd been quiet like this when we were alone, working on our water project. He finally looked at me before dropping his eyes.

At the field the kids crowded around the tree, where a new swing hung from the branch.

"Look, Lucy, it's even better than before!" Becca jumped onto the swing.

"Wow," I said. Two thick chains were bolted to the branch with big silver screws. A long metal bench hung at the end of the chains.

"It's easier," Becca said. "You don't have to squeeze your thighs around the rope."

I turned to Ian. "Did your dad do this?"

"Yeah," Ian said. "It's so sturdy that three people can be on it and it won't break."

"Can I have a turn?" Bucky asked. Ian lifted him onto the bench next to Becca. Bucky and Becca swung back and forth. "Higher, higher!"

There were so many things you couldn't do with the new swing. Twist until you were dizzy. Swing in a big circle. But it did look safer, and learning to hold on wouldn't be as hard.

The other kids giggled as they watched. How long would it be until they forgot about the old swing?

"Let's play chase," Becca said.

"Are you playing?" Peter stood next to Ian.

"Someone has to tell me how." Ian grinned.

"It's like hide-and-seek," Peter said, "only the person finding you has to protect home base. When you get found, you have to stay on base until someone frees you."

"Why not play kick the can?" Ian asked. "That's what it sounds like."

"Because," I said. "We want to use the whole field."

"You can play kick the can in a bigger place," he said.

The kids looked at me, wide-eyed. I frowned and put my hands on my hips.

"Oh, you made it up, so you're the boss, huh?" He saluted me. Peter giggled.

"Don't play if you don't want to," I said.

"No, no, I'm in." He saluted again and everyone laughed. He made me so angry!

"You can be my partner," Bucky said to Ian.

"No, he's mine," Peter said.

I glared at Bucky and Peter. Ian was a hero because his dad had put up a fancy swing?

Becca started counting and everyone bolted. I ran to the back of the Big House. Ian stood behind my favorite hiding tree.

"Ready or not, here I come!" Becca shouted.

I didn't want to hide near Ian, but I had no time to go anywhere else. He crouched behind the tree and I stood over him. He smelled fresh, like the wind. Becca ran past and then it was quiet.

"You run that way," I whispered, pointing left. "I'll go the other way."

"No, I want to go to the right."

"Fine!" I took off. For the next half hour, I found great hiding places. Then I ran to my tree again. I grabbed a low branch, swung my leg over it and climbed until I reached my safe spot. The leaves were good cover and no one had ever found me there.

The spotlight on the back of the Big House crackled and turned on, lighting the dirt below. I watched Peter run past. Then Henry ran by and crouched in the corner where the storage shed connected to the Big House.

After a while I glanced at my watch but it was too dark to see. Superior was terrified of fireworks. I needed to go home. I had just started to climb down when Ian ran up and hid behind the tree. If I jumped down now, he'd know my hiding place.

Minutes ticked by. *Run away, Ian,* I screamed in my head. When a huge sparkling white light exploded over the trees, I jumped down.

"What the . . . !" Ian stumbled backward.

"Sorry." I sprinted past him and met up with Bucky in the field.

"Where were you?" Bucky asked as we ran. "She's gonna be so scared!"

"I know." We raced home. We were in front of our cottage when a second firework lit the sky, white streaks reaching over the bay, then a third. I threw open the door, then ran through the porch and kitchen and up the stairs.

Usually we sat on my rug, Superior trembling between us. I looked in my closet and saw her curled in the corner. Fireworks filled the sky as Bucky and I squished in next to her. I left the door open just a crack.

"I'm so sorry we're late." I stroked her head. She trembled, panting.

The closet was hot and smelled like mildew and wet dog hair. Guilt twisted my stomach. The year before, I'd stayed in bed with the flu for three days and Superior had never left me. Jenny had to put on the leash to get her outside.

Now her body shook; her tongue hung out. Sweat dripped down my back as I fingered the hairs between her toes. We kept talking to her.

"It's hurting her sensitive ears," Bucky said. That was how Dad explained it.

If it hadn't been for Ian, I'd have been here on time. I felt each explosion, deep and painful in my chest. Did Superior feel it there? Maybe we both had big spaces inside us and the explosions filled them up and took over our bodies.

Now the fireworks came quickly. *Boom. Boom!* Finally everything was quiet. But fifteen minutes passed before Superior stopped trembling and we got her downstairs. Outside, the air was cool, the moon bright.

Superior stretched out, rolled onto her back and began wiggling, legs and paws up. I got on my back, too. The grass was wet and cool and tickled my neck. Bucky joined us. Superior started snorting and sneezing, her tail wagging, and we giggled.

We heard the wagon squeak and then Dad came into the backyard. "What's this?"

"Lucy's closet was so hot!" Bucky said.

Dad squatted and rubbed Superior's stomach. "You're the best girl, aren't you?"

"Dad, guess what?" Bucky said. "Ian's dad put up a new swing. It's awesome!"

"I heard," Dad said.

"It's not that great, Buck," I said. "You can't even go in big circles anymore."

"Yeah, but Ian said you could put a bunch of people on it and it won't break. And that it won't ever wear out. And Ian said—"

"So you believe everything Ian says?" I asked.

"I don't know. I kinda like him now."

Great.

I followed Superior as she walked around the yard. When she stopped, I stroked her back. Her coat was as dark as the night and soft and warm.

I looked up. Millions of stars were little white pinpricks in the dark sky, as far as I could see. Below me the dock creaked and the water lapped against the shore and the moored boats.

Back in Boston, when I couldn't sleep, I thought about nights like this up here. Quiet. Beautiful. Peaceful. I took a deep breath, the warm salt air filling my lungs.

I wasn't going to let Ian ruin it.

Chapter 9

Olivia and Lauren wanted to play rescue princess.

"Rescue princess?" I glanced at Peter and his sister, Becca, who were arguing about kickball teams.

"We're princesses, but our evil stepmother put us in an orphanage when our father died." Olivia pointed to the play structure. "You have to rescue us."

"Give me the ball!" Becca yelled. Peter threw it, hitting her in the head. She charged at him, knocking him into the grass.

I ran over and pulled them apart. "Stop!"

"It's her fault," Peter yelled. "She keeps grabbing the ball."

"No, I don't!" Becca said.

"Stop or we won't play at all!" I said. Peter and Becca scowled at each other.

I put home plate near the play structure and split up teams—Bucky, Henry and me versus Becca and Peter. I told the little girls, "Stay on the play structure. I'll rescue you when it's our team's turn to kick."

But the girls kept shouting from the play structure, "Help! Rescue us!" And Peter and Becca argued over who should pitch, who should run for me, who was up first.

Finally I gave up. "Snack time!"

I handed out granola bars, then dropped to the ground, exhausted. Superior was tired, too, from running back and forth with me.

I glanced at my camp schedule. Nothing went as planned.

A truck pulled up. Mr. Richards and Ian got out and examined the porch. Mr. Richards wedged a shovel under a loose shingle on the Big House and pulled, breaking it into a dozen pieces.

I handed out juice boxes, watching until I had to investigate.

Mr. Richards smiled as I walked up. "Ian, it's your friend. What's your name?"

"Lucy," I said. Ian didn't look at me. "What are you doing?"

"I'm looking for water damage, termites. I saw some activity in the crawl space."

"Aren't termites bad?" I asked. Lauren ran up, giggling, and grabbed me.

"Sure. Water damage is, too. If either gets into the supporting beams, we're in big trouble. Might have to replace the beams. Maybe the whole structure."

"But you can't tear it down! The Big House has been here since 1922."

Mr. Richards laughed so loudly that Superior jerked her head to look at him. "You're one of those people, know the dates of everything? My daughter's like you. Knows every-thing, too. We're just checking things out. No need to jump to conclusions."

I glanced down at a huge bucket at their feet, filled with hammers, a saw and other tools.

Mr. Richards's cell phone rang. "Hang on, it's in my truck. Ian, I'll be right back." He walked off.

Peter ran up with the others. "What are you doing?"

"They're going to tear down the Big House!" Lauren said. Everyone gasped.

"That's not what he said." I shook my head. "He doesn't know anything yet."

"But why?" Becca asked.

"Big water damage," Ian said. Everyone looked at him.

"What's that?" Henry pointed to a long, thin metal pole poking out of the bucket.

"This?" Ian grabbed the pole, jumped up and thrust it in front of him. "My sword, and I'm a pirate. I'll cut your heart out and sell it to the first person who pays me!"

He talked in this weird accent as he sliced the air with the pole. "Take that!"

The kids giggled and Peter kept saying, "Do it again!" I put my arms around Olivia and Lauren and pulled them close. He *was* kind of funny, but he could hurt someone if he let go of the pole.

Ian stabbed the air again and again. The kids kept laughing.

"Ian!" Mr. Richards charged over to us. "For God's sake,

70

can't I leave for five minutes without you screwing up? I told you not to touch anything."

Ian's cheeks reddened. I was so surprised that I looked away.

I led the kids back to the field and said, "The Big House is fine. Don't worry!"

I showed them how Superior could catch a tennis ball and they forgot about the Big House. But I kept watching Ian and his dad.

The next couple of days were cold and rainy. On Wednesday we held camp inside the Big House, playing duck, duck, goose and making papier-mâché masks. Peter was bored, but we ended camp with a game of Twister, which he won.

After everyone left, I cleaned up and listened to the rain pound the roof. A cold wind shook the windows and sneaked through the space under the doors. Raindrops fell through the chimney and into the fireplace.

It was hard to imagine that water could cause so many problems.

But after studying it the year before, I knew it did. Water gave life to everything—plants, animals, people—and it could take life away. Countries went to war, people died, over water rights. The ocean could be peaceful one day, violent and destructive the next.

The wind rattled the windows. Dad had lots of memories

of the Big House. Fun times when he was a boy. Most important, asking Mom to marry him after a party.

I had a lot of memories of the Big House, too. Two years earlier Bucky had thrown up on Mrs. Steele during the Welcome Back barbecue. Yow! And I remembered sitting on Mom's lap, watching the talent show.

The talent show was a big tradition. Anyone could perform. The talents varied: singing, juggling and—our favorite, performed by Mr. Ramsey—sucking water from a straw through the nose. Mom had loved the show, too. I would lean into her as we watched and she laughed loud and deep.

I smiled and closed the front door behind me. Rain bounced in the puddles and off the new swing seat.

Superior pricked her ears and we walked to the far side of the porch. Below us Mr. Richards stood in the mud in front of the holes he'd made.

"Hey, just the person I want to see." Water dripped from the bill of his cap.

"Hi."

"My tools are getting wet under the porch. Is there anywhere else I can store them? I don't want to haul them back and forth from home."

"Sure." I pulled up my sweatshirt hood and ran down the steps. I grabbed the small bucket, Mr. Richards took everything else and I led him around the back to the shed, which held old paint cans, a few rakes and garbage cans.

"Perfect." He set everything on the floor. "You'll keep the kids out of here?"

I nodded. "They know the shed is off limits."

He chuckled. "I asked Allison and her new friends what you were doing with all those kids. They said you have a camp, that you're good at being in charge. I like a kid who knows how to work!"

What? The older girls were *talking* about me?

We were soaked, but I didn't care. "Who said I was good at being in charge?"

He started for his truck. "Kiki did, I think. Can't remember exactly. Sorry I can't give you a ride. I'm late for a meeting in town."

"That's okay." I waved as he got into his truck and drove away.

Superior and I headed home. My mind was racing. What else had they said? I floated the entire way back, not minding the rain or the puddles.

Our cottage was quiet and damp. Dad had left me a note. *Bucky is at Henry's and I went into town. Be back at 1.* I dried Superior, put my camp money into my box and sat at Dad's computer.

Mei had emailed me with the best news. Her parents were dropping her off here for a night the next week while they took her older sister to look at colleges in Maine. Hurray! I wrote back, telling her all that we'd do. *Somehow we'll have to avoid Ian (haven't seen him in 2 days). And remember the older girls I told U about? Kiki was telling Mr. Richards about me. So cool. Maybe U could meet her!* I typed.

The house phone rang. "Hello?"

"Hi. Bucky?"

I frowned. The PT. "No, Lucy."

"Oh, Lucy, I'm sorry. It's Julia. I can't hear you. Wait." I heard music and voices in the background but then everything was quiet. "That's better. I'm in a closet now."

"What?"

"I'm at work but there's nowhere to talk, so I'm in a closet. A small utility closet that now smells like Pine-Sol. No wonder. I just tipped over a bottle of it. Hold on."

I didn't want to hold on.

"Well, at least the closet floor is clean."

"My dad isn't here." I tried to sound preoccupied, busy.

"Oh. Maybe I'll try his cell."

"You can't reach him right now." Was that true?

"Okay. Would you tell him that I called and—"

"I gotta go. Bye." I hung up. People didn't have to know where other people were every second of the day.

How much *did* they talk? Every day? Several times a day?

I stomped down the stairs, threw open the door and marched down the road, Superior close behind. Rain pelted my face. All week I'd tried not to think about the PT. She'd be here in two days.

Superior was soaked, her fur dripping water, her ears pulled back. She used to love the rain. She'd leap into puddles and chase frogs.

"I'm sorry, Superior. Let's go back and I'll give you a bath."

She smiled at me with her big dark eyes. But then her ears

pricked up and she turned. Dad's car inched up the road. He stopped and lowered his window. "What are you doing? Get in!"

I climbed into the front seat and put Superior on my lap.

Dad smiled. "Remember how Superior used to run through puddles, not caring whether it was forty degrees or eighty?"

I smiled. "Yeah. She doesn't do that much anymore."

Superior shook, water going everywhere, and we laughed. Then Dad rubbed her chin. "Look how white she's gotten. She's slowing down, isn't she?"

I felt that space open in my chest again. I shook my head. "No, she's the same. I take good care of her."

"Goose, it's not your fault she's getting older."

True, but I was responsible for Superior. And I wasn't going to let her slow down yet.

We watched the rain. Drops the size of nickels hit the windshield, then bounced. Water dripped from my hair onto my neck but I didn't wipe it away. I held my breath, waiting, although I didn't know why.

"Mom liked rain," he said. I nodded. He'd told me this many times. "Sometimes, especially on days like today, I really miss her."

He gripped the steering wheel, staring hard at the rain.

And I felt this deep ache inside me that wanted something so badly I almost couldn't stand it. Was it Mom?

Dad turned to me, his shoulders hunched, his eyes dull. "You're all wet," he said, as if he'd just noticed.

Don't be sad, I thought. I had to do something. "Who, me? I'm not *all wet*. I'm right."

"What?" Then he smiled, slowly. "Oh, I get it. Wise guy."

He put the car in gear and drove slowly around the curve. Wet branches hung over the road. When I saw our cottage, I felt as if I could breathe again. "Are you going to work some more?"

He sat up straighter. "This journal is fascinating. Remember how Thaddeus talked about the fight the Point had with the town over water rights?"

I'd skipped this part because it was so boring.

"Well, Edna has a different take on it. She said it was the *Point's* fault." He chuckled. "I've been looking for a way to arrange everything. Julia had an idea. She said everyone came to the Point looking for something. Don't know why I didn't see that before. It's a great way to organize my material."

My shoulders sank. Why hadn't I thought of that?

"Julia's going to be here in a few days." He stopped in front of the cottage.

I should tell him that she called.

"And, Goose," he said, "you could give her a chance. I really—"

"I've got to give Superior a bath." I jumped out of the car.

Chapter 10

The PT drove a hybrid car, which was good, because that meant she was thinking about the environment. Nothing else about her was good. She was too tall. Her brown hair was too thick, her skin too white. When she smiled, you saw all the way back to her molars.

She shook my hand. Bucky rushed into her arms. Everyone laughed, except me.

"Hello, Superior." The PT stood still, which was good, because Superior didn't like her. The past spring she'd tried to pet Superior, and Superior had growled. Now the PT sighed and looked at the water. "It's so beautiful. Breathtaking, actually."

The birch trees framed the view across the bay. The sun made sparkly silver and blue ripples on the water. *Of course* it was beautiful and breathtaking.

"You gotta see the dock and the beach and the garage."

Bucky pulled on her hand. "Out there is Pear Island and Upper Egg, where we go camping. Every time we go, we get these great hot dogs, special from the market, and we make s'mores, too."

I frowned at him. Why was he telling her all this?

"Whoa, hold on, Buck," Dad said. "We've got time to show her everything."

She laughed, then smiled at me. "Lucy, what do *you* think I should see first?"

I shrugged. How would I know what she'd like? We looked at each other.

"Oh, I brought you something." She leaned into her car.

She handed Dad a jar of jam. "I got this at a wonderful fair yesterday. It's yummy." They smiled at each other. Then she handed a book to Bucky and one to me.

"Thanks," I said. The art historian Dad had dated once brought me a fancy drawing set, but I'd put it in my closet, unopened. I wasn't *that* good of an artist. I glanced at the title, *The Animals of Maine*, and flipped through the torn, yellowed pages. It was a lot like my bird book. I glanced at Dad, but he was looking at her.

"You don't like it?" Her smile faded. "At the fair the library was selling old books and I thought you might . . . Well, I know it's not new. But here, look at this."

She took the book, opened to the inside cover and pulled a white card out of a sleeve. She pointed to the writing at the top: *April 25, 1956. Miss Bingham.*

"Isn't that funny? That people were called Miss? Maybe Miss Bingham was the spinster music teacher at the high school. Or a teenager, like you."

She laughed loudly, then sucked in a breath. No wonder she had trouble breathing. She talked too fast. Dad smiled. Bucky studied the World War II book she'd given him. Maybe I'd look through my book. Later. Before putting it in my closet.

"Can we show Julia the beach?" Bucky asked.

They started down the road. I followed with Superior, my book pressed to my chest. Dad wore a new shirt and shorts. His hair was even combed. He told the PT about the Steeles.

"Tell her about the bow and arrows." Bucky kept jumping as he walked.

Dad nodded. "When I was a kid, Walter would stand on the porch and shoot arrows at targets in the lawn. Scared parents to death. I always knew when he was out, because my dad made me stay inside while he yelled at Walter from our kitchen."

The PT laughed. "He sounds interesting."

She couldn't *possibly* care about this. I ran ahead of them.

At the beach I sat near the water. Soon Dad and the PT walked across the sand and sat near me. I opened my book and turned to a page about wolves, but I couldn't concentrate. I'd never heard Dad talk so much. "I love that restaurant in Portland!" "Work is going well!" "Tell me about that patient from Deer Isle, the man you got to walk again."

She sat with her legs out, her heels digging in the sand.

When she laughed, she threw back her head and her collarbones stuck out. She was too bony. She laughed too much. And Dad laughed too much with her.

Finally they stopped talking. She turned to me and I gripped the sides of my book and focused on the words so hard that they blurred.

"What do you like to do up here, Lucy?"

I didn't look at her. "Stuff."

She hesitated. "Like?"

"Fish."

"Oh, you like to fish? What kind of fish do you catch?"

"All kinds." So many questions!

"Your dad says you're running a camp."

I nodded. I felt Dad's eyes on me but I didn't look at either of them.

"Julia!" Bucky held up a crab. "Come here!"

She walked to Bucky. I went back to the book. *Wolves are carnivores that often prey on big animals. Adult wolves have forty-two razor-sharp teeth, ten more than a human.* No wonder Thaddeus had been afraid when the wolves chased him.

I glanced up and imagined the PT on her hands and knees, all those teeth showing as she chased me around the beach. I shuddered.

"I don't think you're being very friendly," Dad said.

"I'm friendly." But my cheeks stung as I reread the sentence. *Adult wolves have forty-two razor-sharp teeth. Adult wolves have forty-two razor-sharp teeth!*

"You know what I mean."

"I don't feel like talking." I reached for Superior but she was up the beach.

"And you didn't tell me that she called the other day."

"Sorry. I forgot."

Dad was quiet, then sighed. "I know this is hard. But you need . . . Well. She's just a wonderful person, Goose. You don't have to be worried. And . . ."

"I'm not worried!" I left the book in the sand and walked to the rocks.

Bucky was teaching the PT how to hold the crab. I imagined her crushing the crab. She turned it around, staring at it from all sides before handing it back to Bucky.

We walked back to the cottage. Bucky ran off with Henry and I put the book in my room. Then I sat at my puzzle. Dad and the PT were in the kitchen, talking as *pop!* a cork came out of a wine bottle. I kept glancing at the door. Were they talking about me?

"This looks like a tough one," the PT said from the doorway. Dad sat on the couch and picked up the newspaper.

"May I?" She pointed to the chair next to me. I shrugged. She tried to sit, only she stepped on Superior, who was lying under the table, and jumped back, knocking my water bottle onto the floor.

"Oh! I didn't see her! I'm so sorry." She looked under the table. "Are you okay?"

I lifted Superior's paw, examining it closely. She was okay, but I kissed it twice. The PT sighed, picked up my water bottle and put it on the table.

"Let's try this again." She sat and stared at the puzzle. "Your dad says a boy from your school moved up here."

If I stayed quiet, would she *leave*?

"That must feel strange, someone from back home suddenly living here."

How did *she* know? I tried forcing a blue puzzle piece into the sky but it wouldn't fit. I felt her staring at me, waiting.

"That's enough, Lucy." Dad's voice was angry.

"Oh, Ben, don't, it's okay," she said.

I pushed back my chair, ran to the door and threw it open. I took the stairs two at a time to the dock. I sat and hung my legs over the edge, the water cold and numbing.

Jenny probably would say, "It's good your dad has a friend." But this wasn't like the art historian. Something felt different.

The air was still, the water calm. A sailboat motored toward the marina, its sails tied to the mast. Someone in a kayak hugged the coast, silently paddling toward me.

The stairs creaked. Superior came down first, nuzzled my neck, then sat. Dad followed, frowning. He was hardly ever mad at me. I wrapped my arms around my knees and pulled them into my chest. Now the cold water on my legs numbed my arms, too.

Dad squatted next to me, frown fading. "You're upset."

The kayak was closer now. Mrs. Ramsey waved from it and Dad and I waved back.

"You don't have to feel threatened," Dad said.

I wasn't threatened! Or worried or anything except . . . Except what?

"She asks too many questions. I don't like her!" There, I'd said it. But I felt a sting in my chest. Lines creased his forehead.

"Hi!" Mrs. Ramsey paddled to the dock. Her kayak was shiny green with a black racing stripe across the top. The cockpit fit snugly around her. "I saw an eagle!"

"What?" Dad stood. "Where?"

"By the beach. Beautiful, soaring up into the nest. Only one of them, though."

Dad nodded. "The other is probably staying in the nest."

"You're welcome to use my kayak."

"Thanks, but I can't today." Dad touched the hull. "Such a beaut!"

"Are you sure, Ben? I know how much you like it. What about you, Lucy?"

"No, thanks," I said. We talked for a while and she paddled off silently. *Such a beaut.* The kayak I'd picked for Dad in my boating magazine was just as nice.

He cleared his throat. "All I'm asking is that you give Julia a chance."

He didn't ask me to *like* her.

"Okay."

* * *

After dinner, we played Monopoly. When it was time for bed, Bucky hugged the PT before heading upstairs. I waved from the doorway.

I tucked Bucky in and counted the money in my box. Then Superior settled on my rug and I got into bed. I stared at the ceiling and listened to muffled voices on the porch.

During dinner the PT had told us that at her job she treated people who had been injured or had surgery. She often had to help people learn to live with what had happened to them, such as this guy who'd torn up his knee and couldn't play football. I listened, feeling okay.

A cool breeze blew through my window. I heard laughter and glanced at *The Animals of Maine* on the floor. It was a decent present.

I reached down and touched Superior. Back home when I couldn't sleep, I played a game from bed, pretending that my ceiling was a new country and the cracks were roads and rivers. I kept adding new details. The ceiling fan was a terrifying whirlpool, the streak marks above my bureau a dangerous waterfall. I had to find my way around it all.

But this ceiling didn't have cracks. And I didn't usually lie awake so long here.

Finally, at midnight, I heard voices outside. Soon Dad climbed the stairs. I closed my eyes and felt him at the door. Then the floor creaked and he was gone. I rolled onto my back, listening to water running in the bathroom and Dad humming.

The PT made him happy.

84

Chapter 11

The next morning I stood at the counter, staring at two wineglasses in the sink, one with red lipstick on the rim. What had they talked about the night before? Mom?

I tried to think about something happy, like Mei's visit, as I washed the glasses. The lipstick was gone but I couldn't stop thinking about Mom.

She'd died from a stage four glioblastoma. I didn't know these words until later. At first, everyone called it cancer. Rhymed with *dancer*. The beginning sounded like the first part of *Kansas*.

One day Mom was fine, the next day she had cancer and a year later she was gone. In between, there were treatments, surgery and hospitals, although it was all pretty hazy in my mind. And it never made sense. How could a little tumor have killed my mom?

Then one day this year, Jenny looked up from the newspaper. "This guy died from a glioblastoma, like your mom."

I'd heard the word before. But it wasn't until I looked it up on the Internet that I knew exactly what it was: the most malignant of the astrocytomas, which are star-shaped brain tumors.

Malignant. Glioblastoma. Astrocytomas. Blaming such big, ugly words for what happened to Mom made me feel better. Although sometimes when I said them, I felt a twinge, like what happened when you had to keep reminding yourself that there was no such thing as ghosts.

"Good morning!" Dad grinned as he walked into the kitchen. Bucky and I mumbled hello through mouthfuls of cereal.

As Dad made coffee, he said, "Enjoy the sunshine. Rain is supposed to start this afternoon."

I groaned. Camp was much easier outside. And I didn't want any more water damage to the Big House.

"So, what did you think about yesterday?" he asked. "Julia?"

"I like her!" Bucky waved his spoon. I frowned at him but he didn't notice.

"She likes you, too. And she really likes it here."

I glanced at the clock: a half hour until camp. Afterward Superior and I were headed to the beach so I could finish my eagle drawing.

"What did you think, Goose?"

Don't make him angry, I thought. I shrugged.

"I really, really like her, guys." Dad smiled as he poured a cup of coffee. I started for the porch before he could go on.

"Come on, Superior, Buck," I called. "Time to go."

* * *

The rain started that night. By Wednesday morning at breakfast, everything was soaked. The cottage was damp and sticky and towels wouldn't dry. Waterlogged tree branches dipped over the road, and a giant puddle covered the walkway.

"You can call off camp," Dad said.

I shook my head. "Friendship bracelets," I said, showing him my bag filled with colored string. The boys wouldn't like making bracelets, and it might be hard for the little ones, but I'd help.

Dad gave me a hug. "Those kids are lucky to have you."

I leaned against him for a second, my head resting on his chest.

"Let's go." Bucky poked me.

By eleven the rain had stopped, but it was too muddy to go outside. We'd used the last of the paints and made bracelets. Everybody started running around, and Becca skidded on Poley, Lauren's stuffed polar bear, tearing off her leg.

Stuffing fell out of Poley's leg when I picked her up. I knelt in front of Lauren, who was crying. "I bet your mom can sew it."

She looked at me hopefully. "If I wish hard, Poley's leg will grow back on."

Wishes *could* come true. When I'd wished for a dog, Dad had brought Superior home. I took Lauren's hand and walked to the porch. "Look how pretty it is now!"

The sun, peeking through the clouds, made the puddle on the swing seat sparkle. The air smelled like pine and freshly cut grass.

"Boo!"

I jumped. Ian came around the corner, his sneakers covered in mud, his gym shorts hanging past his knees. Lauren giggled, and I laughed, just a little. "You scared me."

Ian looked over my shoulder into the Big House. The older kids were still chasing each other. Olivia, on her hands and knees, barked at Superior, who ate pretzels off the floor. "Pretty exciting camp."

"We're taking a break."

"Ian, watch this!" Peter ran across the floor and knocked Becca into the wall. But not too hard.

"Nice check!" Ian yelled. The kids kept running as Superior trotted over to us.

"She always knows where you are," Ian said, squatting. Superior stepped toward him.

"Come here!" She turned and sat next to me. I glanced at my watch. "Okay, time to clean up!"

Everyone groaned. But for the next couple of minutes, we stuffed newspapers, juice boxes and pretzel bags into the trash. Ian stayed on the porch while everyone left.

I was closing the door when Dad came across the field. He raised his arms. "The sun, finally! Hello, Ian. Nice to see you."

"Nice to see you, Dr. Gallagher." Ian thrust his hand out. Dad shook it. "Call me Ben."

"Thanks. I was wondering how the book is coming along.

That's pretty impressive, knowing so much about something that you could write a book about it."

I rolled my eyes. Such a suck-up!

Dad grinned. "Well, I don't know . . ."

"I'd sure like to hear more about it sometime," Ian said.

"Time to go." I started down the steps, two at a time.

"Hold on. It'll be a bit muddy but I came over to see if you want to go out to Pear." Dad turned to Ian. "It's our favorite island. Want to come?"

My eyes jumped out of their sockets. *Not Ian!*

"Sure, okay!" Ian grinned.

"Go clear it with your folks, then meet us at our dock."

Ian took off through the field. As Dad and I started back to the cottage, I walked ahead, my arms pumping at my sides, my face and body hot.

"So, I guess I shouldn't have asked him?" Dad caught up to me. "You're the only kid his age here, Goose. I was trying to be nice."

"I know." I kept walking. Dad would see soon enough who Ian really was.

We made sandwiches and filled a cooler with sodas, then carried everything to the boat, where Ian was waiting. I untied the ropes and we were off. I sat next to Dad, protected by the windshield, where I could hold on to the side of the boat.

Ian stood next to Dad, asking questions. What did that lever do? And that gauge? How far was it to Pear? How fast would the boat go? What kind of gas did it take?

Every time we hit a wave, my stomach leaped. Ian wasn't

afraid of the water. Neither were Dad and Bucky. Superior was in the back, barking at the wake. She wasn't afraid, either. It was her game. *I'll get you! And you!*

I glanced across the bay. Two years earlier an author had given a workshop at our school and told us to write about a time when we were afraid.

At first I didn't know what to write. Then I thought about Katie Recht's sixth birthday party, at her pool with the big blue slide, and how I'd really wanted to go. It had been hot that day and I'd been happy to be there, not at the hospital seeing Mom.

And I remembered not being able to breathe.

So I figured that I must have gone down that slide and landed wrong in the water. And maybe *that* had knocked the air out of me. That was why I'd felt as if I were sinking. And that was why Dad had carried me to the car while Mrs. Recht had cried.

But this was where everything got confusing, because Dad was supposed to be at the hospital. And I still couldn't quite picture the pool in my mind.

But I remembered the feeling of not being able to breathe, so that was what I wrote about. How scared I'd been when I'd nearly drowned in the Rechts' pool.

Now I held on tight as the boat bounced in the water.

Finally Dad slowed, cut the engine and threw out the anchor. We waded to shore, then sat and ate our sandwiches, our feet and legs drying in the hot sun.

I couldn't stop watching Ian and noticing things about

him. How he took huge bites of his sandwich. How long and thin his fingers were, wrapped around the bread. How everything was familiar—the boat ride, the cold prickles on my legs, the sand—but *felt* different with him here.

Dad and Bucky wandered up the shore, turning over rocks, looking for crabs.

Ian wadded his waxed paper and tossed it into the cooler. "Score!"

He smiled at me, a big toothy grin that made me smile back. Then we both looked away.

"Let's go to the top of the hill!" Bucky yelled. Ian and I jumped up and followed.

The path was narrow and we walked uphill single file. Dad kept turning to Ian, behind Bucky. "This is an oak, one of Maine's most common foliage trees. Down there, blueberry bushes. Soon they'll be crawling with wild blueberries."

"You can eat them?" Ian asked. Dad nodded.

Ian grinned at me again, only this time it seemed more like a smirk. He was two different people—one way with me, another with adults.

A half hour later we reached the top of the hill, an open, grassy area that faced the bay between Pear and the Point. The wind was strong, the water choppier and a deeper blue than when we'd come over.

"Ian, look!" Bucky called from the far side of the clearing. Ian ran over and they looked at something in the grass. Superior sat next to me.

Dad laughed. "He's a funny kid. Lots of energy."

"He's a huge suck-up, Dad."

"Hmmm. But his enthusiasm is infectious. Don't you think?"

Infection? Yes.

"He's interested in boats, history. He seems like a hard worker." Dad cleared his throat. "The talent show is next weekend."

"I can't wait!"

"I want to ask Julia to come up."

I whipped my head to look at him. "But she was just here."

"I miss her. We have very deep feelings for each other, Goose."

My stomach turned.

"She's a nice person. And, well, we have a lot in common. I'd like to see her more, for all of us to see her more."

I was so angry I was afraid to look at him.

He waited. "Why don't you like her? Do you think your feelings about her are . . . about Mom?"

"No!" How could he put the PT in the same *sentence* as Mom?

"I just wish . . . ," he said. "Oh, Goose, you don't have to be so worried."

"Stop telling me that!"

Bucky yelled, "Lucy! Come look!" I bolted from the spot.

Chapter 12

We planned to meet Mei's family fifteen minutes away, at the Dunkin' Donuts near the highway, and bring Mei back to the Point. We got there first. I couldn't wait!

When she arrived, we jumped out of our cars and hugged. She was dressed just like me, in flip-flops, shorts and a T-shirt. She bent over and held out her hand to Superior, who sniffed, then moved next to me.

We said good-bye to her family, then climbed into our car, Superior between us. Most of the times when Mei came to our house, Dad was working, so they didn't really know each other.

For some reason, I felt nervous. Maybe she was, too, because we couldn't stop laughing at little things.

When Superior squeaked as she yawned, we doubled up, hysterical.

"Am I missing something?" Dad glanced in the rearview mirror.

That cracked us up, too.

But when Dad turned onto the dirt road and we drove through the tunnel of pine trees, Mei lowered her window, watching, quiet. I pointed to the Grahams' cottage, and the Dennises', then the Debacle.

When we rounded the bend, I said, "There's our cottage."

She squeezed my arm. "There's the ocean! Lucy, it's so awesome!"

Dad turned and grinned at me. He liked Mei; I could tell.

We dumped Mei's stuff in my room and packed lunch into my backpack. Then Superior and I showed her the Big House, the swampy woods, the path to town and the beach. We climbed over the rocks, looking for crabs and running our fingers over the snails.

The wind was so strong that it blew our hair sideways. Superior barked at the waves that splashed onto the rocks at our feet. We sat and tried to eat lunch, although the wind nearly tore the sandwiches from our hands.

Mei stood and spread her arms wide. "It's gonna blow me away!"

I laughed. "You're too heavy."

"I can pretend." She closed her eyes and tipped back her head. The wind tangled her hair and puffed out her shirt. "Come on, let's be birds."

She flapped her arms up and down, like wings. I glanced around; no one was here except us. I stood and started flapping my arms, too. Then a big wave hit the rocks, sending a cold spray all over us, and we screamed and burst out laughing.

Finally I picked up my backpack and we started toward the shore.

"Show me Ian's house, up close," she said.

I shook my head. There was nowhere to hide if he caught us in his backyard. We walked up the beach to the path.

"I can't come here and not see his house," Mei said. "And the new dock."

If we went through the Dennises' backyard, maybe we could avoid him. "Okay."

We walked down the road, turning at the bend. The De-bacle stood ahead, covered in shadows from nearby trees. We passed it, then circled back behind the Dennises' cottage. We stopped at a birch tree that bordered the two properties and watched.

"I don't think anyone's home," I said. Mei walked around the tree and into Ian's yard. I followed. The windows were closed, blinds drawn.

"The dock is huge," she said. "And look at all the windows."

"Yeah, but do you think it fits in?" I asked.

"Hello? Not!"

We giggled.

"Let's go," I said. This time we walked up Ian's yard and along the side of his garage. I was so close that I dragged my fingers on the shingles. The garage door opened just as we started around the corner.

We screamed, then pressed our backs against the wall. Superior barked at us and wouldn't stop.

Ian walked around the side. "What are you doing?"

Mei pulled away but I sank to my knees, holding Superior, who licked my face.

"Oh, hi, Ian," Mei said.

"Why are you here?" He glared at me.

"I'm visiting Lucy," she said.

"No, I mean, what are you doing at my house?"

"I was just showing her around." I stood. "The beach, the Dennises' cottage, your new dock and stuff."

"Oh." We just stood there, not looking at each other.

"We should go," I said. "Bye."

"Bye!" Mei said.

"See ya," Ian said.

We walked down the driveway. Once on the road, we ran, trying not to laugh, and didn't stop until we rounded the bend.

"Whoa, that was awkward." I sucked in big breaths.

"Yeah, but he was okay."

I looked at her. Annoying. Jerk. Back home, those were just two of the names she called him. But she was right. We'd been spying and he could have been awful about it.

Later Dad cooked lobsters out back, next to the picnic table. Bucky showed Mei how to crack the shells—she'd never had a lobster before—and we all cracked up when she accidentally flung a claw across the table at him.

Then we roasted marshmallows over the fire pit and

looked for shooting stars. Mei and I were exhausted when we finally crawled into sleeping bags. Superior, her back squished to mine, fell asleep instantly. Mei and I listened as the wind stirred the boats and the trees and shook my screens.

"I could pretty much live up here," Mei said. "Even with Ian."

"He was okay today."

"But usually he's *so* annoying. Right?"

"Right." I sighed and thought about the last time Mei and I had talked, on the bus while visiting the middle school. "Are you still dreading Duggan?"

"My parents are getting me a math tutor, so I guess that'll help."

Up here I hadn't thought much about school. But it was only six weeks away.

For now, everything was perfect.

In the morning I had just enough time to show Mei one more place.

We ran past the swamp, through the parking lot, then up the wooden stairs to the dock outside the marina store. The air was warm, and the salty smell so strong you could almost taste it.

Below us an old fishing boat was tied to a post. Pete, the marina owner, and Jake Ramsey stacked lobster traps on the dock. Mei watched, her mouth falling open.

I laughed. "Those are just lobster cages."

"No." Mei shook her head. "Who's that cute guy?"

"Jake Ramsey, Henry's brother."

Jake stood straight and stretched. He wore jeans and no shirt and his tan muscles glistened in the sun. He *was* great-looking, even though he was old. He went to college and had a summer job in Boston, so he was only here on weekends. I used to imagine that he and Kiki would get married someday but Dad said they were just good friends.

I walked over to the window and looked into the store. Kiki, the real reason I'd brought Mei here, stood behind the counter. I whispered, "Kiki's here."

Mei hurried over. Kiki was making something with red tissue paper. She wore a blue Pete's Marina T-shirt and her long red hair was pulled into a ponytail.

Most kids on the Point wanted to work at Pete's when they got older, but only a few ever got the best job: manning the counter. You had to work your way up, cleaning traps and doing yard work.

Kiki turned her head toward us and we dropped to the deck, giggling.

"Let's go in," Mei said.

It was the perfect chance. Kiki was alone. "Okay."

I told Superior to sit—she wasn't allowed in—and opened the door. A blast of cold air from the air conditioner blew back our hair.

"Hey, Lucy!" Kiki looked down at the flower she was making out of tissues.

"Hey." Buckets of candy lined the shelf under the counter. When I was younger, I loved filling a bag, then eating the candy as Dad, Mom and I walked back to the cottage.

"What's going on?"

"This is my friend Mei. She's visiting from Boston."

"Hi." Kiki smiled. "Is this your first time at the Point?"

Mei nodded.

The door opened and an elderly man came in. "Hey, Kiki."

"Hey, Mr. Selfors. You get something down below?"

"Yep, five lobsters, one pound each."

Kiki rang him up at the register. "I heard your wife's sick."

"She's better," he said. They talked about his wife and the weather. Then he thanked her and left.

I didn't exactly know what I wanted. I just felt good around Kiki. "What are you making?"

"Don't you think we need some color? I'm going to put them on the shelves." Kiki held up the flower. It was thick and full, like a blossoming rose. She put it on the shelf behind her, next to the mousetraps and scouring pads. It looked perfect.

"Yes," I said. "It must be fun working here."

She nodded. Everything about her was great—her smooth skin, her green eyes, her chipped fingernail polish. I brought my hand up to my sore ears and twisted my earrings. Kiki started to make another flower.

Mei elbowed me, then mouthed, *Tell her about your camp.*

I nodded. "So, you know I'm running this camp? Well, it's pretty fun."

Kiki scrunched up her nose, as if she didn't know what I

was talking about, then slowly smiled. "Oh, yeah. That's so cool. You should feel proud of yourself."

I wanted to tell her *everything*. That I was saving to buy a kayak for my dad. That science was my favorite subject. That someday I'd work at the marina, too.

But Mary, Pete's wife, called from the back room. "Need you back here, Kiki. Meat to slice."

"Coming. It was nice to meet you, Mei. Have fun." And then she disappeared into the back room.

We started back to the cottage, my feet barely touching the ground.

"She's nice," Mei said. "She thought your camp was so cool."

I grinned.

We were out of the woods and on the road when we heard Dad yell for us. We ran. Then it was time to take Mei to meet her parents.

We hugged extra hard in the Dunkin' Donuts parking lot. As I watched the car drive away, I didn't want her to go.

"That went well, huh?" Dad said as we drove back to the Point.

"It was great."

"She's a good friend," he said. "I hope she can come back."

"Yes!" I looked out the window. You could do so much with a good friend. Be silly on the rocks. Talk to the most annoying boy on the planet. Laugh and laugh.

Maybe the next time I saw Kiki, I wouldn't be nervous.

Chapter 13

I sat at the computer, staring out the window. A mist hung over the water, then thickened farther out so you didn't know what you were seeing. Could have been a pond or a river. Could have been Lake Superior.

Mom had grown up on Lake Superior, which was so big Dad said it looked like the ocean. I'd been there once, but I'd been too young to remember. Dad said he and Mom had walked the beach after a storm. The water had been so rough that it had churned up iron ore in the sand, making the waves red.

At home, we had a photo of Mom and Dad on the lake; it looked just like the open ocean off Pierson Point.

When Dad turned off the shower, I ducked into my room. I knew he wanted to talk about the PT. I grabbed my notebook and bird book, and Superior and I headed over to babysit at the Dennises'.

Lauren and Stevie were waiting at the door. After their mom left, Lauren flipped through my notebook, pointing to her favorite drawings. Then we walked down to their dock to draw. The fog had begun to burn off; the tide was high, the water still.

Lauren drew Priscilla, a magical horse who talked and lived in the woods between here and town. She colored the horse purple. "She eats corn and hay."

"If she lives in the woods, where does she get corn and hay?" I asked.

"She wishes and it comes."

Stevie nodded, and I laughed. Had I had such a big imagination when I was their age?

The past summer I'd been able to see way out into the bay, but now the new dock next door blocked my view. I closed my eyes, trying to remember how it had looked, then opened them when I heard a splash. Allison bobbed to the surface next door.

She swam to us, climbed the ladder and stood, dripping water.

"You're all cold." Lauren pointed to Allison's legs, covered in goose bumps.

"No, I'm not," she said.

Lauren darted a look at me.

Allison shivered as she leaned over Lauren. "What's that?"

"It's Priscilla, a magical talking horse. She lives in the woods over there."

"Right." Allison looked at me but I closed my notebook and bird book. "Let's see."

I sighed and showed her my eagle.

She studied it. "Not bad. Nice beak and the eyes work. Put the book away. You don't need to copy. Just draw from what's in your brain."

"I'm not good at drawing from my imagination."

"Sure you are. I took a couple of classes. I'll help you. But I'm going to be pretty busy. Ian, too. He's going to sailing camp. I'm so insanely bored that I got a job at the marina."

I sat up and smiled. "Kiki works there."

"Yeah, she's got the easy job, working inside. I have to work in the yard."

I nodded. "Everyone has to start outside. But the harder you work, the easier it is to move up. Kiki's been behind the counter for two summers now."

Allison tilted her head and stared at me. Had I said something wrong?

"Anyway, wish I'd started today," she said. "Before Ian's idiot friend arrives."

"Who's coming?" I asked.

"When Ian and his friends are around, they take over. My mom lets them get away with *anything*." She raised her eyebrows. "What's he like in class? Annoying? Obnoxious?"

Ian was both of those things, but who cared right now? Who was coming?

"Come on." Allison gathered her long hair behind her. Silver studs sparkled in her ears. "Give me some inside scoop."

"I don't know him . . ."

"You're protecting him." She laughed. "*Everyone* protects him. Just know that he's not so nice the other way around."

"What do you mean?"

"He said he knows *you.*"

"What did he say?"

"You don't want to know." She dove into the water, then swam away on her back, grinning. "Just kidding!"

Was she?

"Let's go," I said. We gathered the markers and paper and I marched the kids up to the cottage. I wanted to punch something. Did he tell lies about me to his family, too?

We sat in the kitchen and ate Popsicles, both kids on my lap. Lauren told another story about Priscilla, but I barely listened. The talent show was that weekend. Ian and his friend—maybe Michael?—would probably stand in the back of the Big House, making fun of everything.

If only Mei were still here!

Chapter 14

The PT wore the ugliest bathing suit I'd ever seen, blue with big yellow sunflowers. I couldn't stop looking at it as we all stood on the dock, waiting for Mr. Ramsey to take us tubing. She talked about how beautiful the Point was, how she'd never been tubing. Every time she laughed, her shoulders shook and the sunflowers bounced.

"I'm nervous. Lucy, do you have any pointers?" she asked. Dad smiled at me.

"No," I said. Then I stomped up to the cottage.

I sat at the computer and wrote Mei, telling her that Ian had a friend here, although I didn't know who. Then I pushed away from the computer and picked up Dad's manuscript.

Eagles were such a big deal on the Point that Dad had given them a whole chapter. I read about how they mate for life and return to their nests every spring to make them stronger for their babies. Dad had written in the margin *How quickly does eagle find new mate after first mate dies?*

I stopped reading.

If an eagle mates for life, how can it just go out and find a replacement?

I jumped up and went to my room, Superior behind me. I threw myself on my bed, burying my face in my quilt.

A sob filled my chest. Dad was in love with the PT.

Would they get married? A girl from school said that when her dad remarried, her stepmom repainted the whole house and got new furniture.

I loved the leather couch in our living room back in Boston, even with the screwdriver holes in the cushion. And I wouldn't let her fix the cracks on my bedroom ceiling.

If they got married, she'd live up here, too. In our cottage.

Superior put her nose on my bed and I reached over and rubbed her head, closing my eyes. I must have dozed off, because when I opened them, the sun was shining across my floor at a different angle. Superior was asleep on the rug.

I wiped my sweaty forehead on my quilt and watched it turn a checked octagon dark blue. Dad said this piece of the quilt came from a bandanna Mom had worn. I knew where every octagon came from. The S on the gray background was from Mom's Smith College shirt. The pink flowers were from her sundress. The denim was from her jeans.

A knock.

"Lucy?" The PT. I stuffed the quilt into a ball and opened the door.

Her long white arms and legs were splotchy with sunburn

and she wore red lipstick that made her mouth look huge. In her ears were silver hoop earrings. I brought my hand to my right ear and twisted my stud.

"I'm sorry to bother you," she said.

"It's okay." But I didn't invite her in.

"I know this sounds crazy, but . . . Well, I think someone is spying on the cottage."

This was the last thing I'd expected. She walked in and leaned over my desk to look out the window. I leaned next to her. The lotion she had on smelled like herbs, the kind Mrs. Steele grew in her garden.

"The first couple times they walked by slowly, looking at the cottage. Then they stood behind a tree and watched. Now, where are they? There, behind that tree. Look!"

Ian and Charlie stood behind a pine tree, looking around it at our cottage.

"That's Ian and Charlie."

"Ian's the new boy?"

I nodded and stepped back so they couldn't see me. They shoved each other, laughing, then walked away. We watched until they were out of sight. I wished Mei had come up that weekend, too.

"Is Ian shy?" the PT asked.

"No. He's popular and I'm . . . He never talks to me. Except . . . Well, he teases everyone, not just me. I don't know why they came over here." This was the most I'd ever said to her.

"Maybe he likes you."

My eyes popped out. Mei and I had done the same thing, spied on Ian, and not because we liked him. "No, you don't know Ian." But I watched her, my heartbeat quickening.

"True." She put her hands on her hips, then began spinning a pencil on my desk. "I was thinking about a boy, Doug Henney, but everyone called him Harry Hen. In sixth grade he used to unhook the rubber bands in his braces and shoot them at me."

I smiled. Harry Hen sounded like a name Dad and I would make up.

"So, I saw him at a class reunion not too long ago and he said he'd had a crush on me since first grade. Shocked me to death." She laughed, still spinning the pencil.

She wouldn't be here if she'd married Harry Hen, would she? Dad said she'd been married before.

"Sometimes what seems to be one thing turns out to be another." She spun the pencil so fast that it flew off the desk and landed on Superior. "I'm sorry, Superior." She reached for the pencil, then quickly drew back her hand.

Superior didn't move. I put the pencil back on my desk. Maybe the PT wasn't so much clumsy as something else. What?

I leaned over my desk and looked out the window again. No Ian. The PT smiled and pointed to my ears. "They're a little red. Do they still hurt?"

I hesitated. The week before, I'd emailed Jenny about my swollen earlobes and she'd written back *I'm all thumbs with things of fashion. Tell your dad!* But I didn't, because then he'd worry. "Kinda. But I take care of them."

"Come with me." In the bathroom she pulled a small bottle out of a flowered bag. She poured from the bottle onto a cotton ball, gently pushed down the back of my earring and pressed the cotton ball to my skin.

"It's rubbing alcohol. The trick is to make sure you pull down the earring so the alcohol gets inside," she said. "Otherwise you're only treating the outside."

I nodded. "Is this normal, that they still hurt? I've been putting stuff on them."

She held the cotton ball to my other ear. "Everyone's different, but I think mine hurt for a month or so. I remember sleeping on my back because having my ears against the pillow kept waking me."

Just like me.

"So just keep putting alcohol on them," she said.

"Thanks."

She smiled. "You're welcome."

We stood there, looking everywhere but at each other. When she left, I locked the door, turned on the shower and stared at myself in the mirror.

I had freckles on my nose, lips that were too thin and extra-long eyelashes. Nothing else about me stood out. Not like Annie, with her long blond hair and blue eyes. The boys thought she was really pretty. The PT was wrong. Ian didn't like me.

I opened her flowered bag. Lipstick, mascara, bandages,

toothpaste, mouthwash, lotion. I unzipped a smaller bag and pulled out a pair of gold hoop earrings.

I held them to my ears. I liked how the gold looked against my brown hair. They made me seem older, at least Allison's age. I put them back and unscrewed the cap on the lotion bottle. Strong, clean. Like the PT.

What kind of lotion had Mom used? I remembered the loose rings on her finger and how her hair fell on her shoulders. But I couldn't remember her smell. I put the lotion back and moved the bag to the floor, where I wouldn't see it anymore.

Time to get ready for the talent show.

Chapter 15

The temporary boards that had been on the Big House had been pulled off and now there was a gaping hole next to the stairs. Someone had blocked off the area with yellow tape.

I ran up the stairs. People had already filled the chairs lined up in front of the fireplace. Others stood along the sides. Kiki sat squeezed between Tonya and Danielle on a table in the back of the room. They swung their legs underneath them.

I walked through the crowd until I was only a few feet away from them. When Kiki turned toward me and smiled, I raised my hand. "Hi!" Maybe I could sit with them.

But then Jake jumped onto the table next to Danielle. They all started talking.

Lauren ran up and pulled my arm. "Lucy, sit with me."

"I will, just a minute," I said. Lauren ran off.

"You like them." Allison stood next to me.

My cheeks got red, but Allison wasn't laughing at me. "Yeah, of course."

"You could hang with us sometime."

"Okay, thanks."

Allison sat next to Tonya.

"Let's get started," Mr. Ramsey said into the micro-phone. When I sat next to Lauren, Stevie crawled into my lap.

Ian and Charlie leaned against the wall, whispering, laughing. Would they do that through the show? When Mei had been here, we laughed the whole weekend.

Lauren was first. She sang "Over the Rainbow," smiling at her mom and dad. She was great and Stevie and I high-fived her when she finished. Becca played her violin and Jake Ramsey juggled tennis balls. Mrs. Graham showed her paintings, Mr. Dennis told a really bad joke and the Averys sang the Cornell fight song.

I glanced back at the older girls. What would Allison say to them about me?

"Okay, anyone else?" Mr. Ramsey said. This was a perfect place for Ian to show off. But he just kept whispering to Charlie.

"Lucy!" Becca and Peter pulled on my arm. She said, "We're playing chase, right?"

"My cousins are here, so they're playing," Peter said. "And Ian and his friend."

Everyone shushed them.

"I guess I'm last." Mr. Ramsey put a straw in a glass of water, then stuck the other end up his nose. He breathed in and the water disappeared up the straw into his nose. Everyone screamed with laughter.

"And that's the end of our show," Mr. Ramsey said. "We don't usually do business here, but we need to talk about something. Kids, you don't have to stay."

Was this about the Big House? Ian and Charlie walked out behind the older girls. I wanted to listen but I didn't want them playing without me.

Outside, the younger kids stood by the swing with Charlie and Ian. It was dusk but the lawn was lit from the Big House lights and the hundreds of stars in the sky. Lauren cupped a firefly in her hands and peeked inside them.

"Hey," Charlie and I said to each other. He was tall and skinny, like Ian, with black hair. I'd known him forever.

I explained the rules.

"I don't get it," Charlie said. "Why do you have to team up to free someone?"

"Makes it harder for the person who's it," I said.

"Ian, can I be it?" Peter asked. "Okay?"

"Hey!" Why didn't he ask me?

"Sure." Ian grinned at me. Peter started to count and we scattered.

Peter captured Lauren and me, and we waited in jail until Ian and Charlie freed us. Peter's cousins never got caught.

113

That night was super fun. No one wanted to stop, not even when the lights were turned off in the Big House.

The air was warm and muggy, the crickets and bullfrogs loud. Sweat dripped down my back as I ran along the road to the far side of the bushes. Charlie grabbed my arm, pulling me behind a bush, where he hid with Ian. I crouched behind them. Through an opening in the leaves, we saw Becca guarding the jail in front of the Big House stairs.

"She's got everyone else," Ian whispered.

"We gotta come up with a plan." Charlie slapped at a mosquito on his neck.

"Let's sneak around the back," Ian whispered. "Then run out, a full blitz."

"If we do that, Becca can just call our names and we're caught," I whispered. "I'll go around the long way, come out on the path and make a noise. She'll come toward me; then you guys run around the back and free everyone."

"You'll be a decoy," Charlie said. "Brilliant."

"It's not *that* brilliant," Ian grumbled.

We were quiet and then a voice behind us said, "What are you *doing?*"

We jumped. It was so dark that I could barely make out Allison's face.

"Shush!" Ian said.

"*Please,*" she said. "You act like you're five. Lucy, I'm surprised at you."

"We're just playing a game," I said.

"Then again, I barely ever see you without your posse."

114

She chuckled. "Ian, did you know Lucy and I are friends? She's an artist and I'm gonna teach her some tricks. Let's go, Lucy."

Go? I wanted to stay.

"Just do a blitz," Ian said.

"What is this, capture the flag?" Allison asked.

"Kind of," I said. "We have to free everyone without Becca seeing us."

"If you do a blitz, you'll all get caught," Allison said. "Split up and distract her while one of you frees everyone."

"That's what Lucy said," Charlie replied.

"Shut up," Ian said.

"This isn't fun anymore!" Becca yelled.

"*I'll* be the decoy." Ian ran behind us, along the road and into the woods.

The moon was a giant white circle in the sky. Mosquitoes buzzed in my ears. Fireflies flashed, then disappeared.

"This is boring. I'm out of here." Allison sighed and walked into the dark.

Charlie and I were quiet, watching, waiting. He slapped at a mosquito again. "You're friends with Allison?"

I stared into the dark, to make sure she was gone. "Kind of."

"Oh. Don't you think she's a jerk to Ian?"

"Maybe he deserves it."

"Really?"

I didn't want to argue. Of course he'd stick up for Ian. Allison was nice to me.

"I see you!" Becca yelled, and took off across the field.

Charlie and I ran around the bush, yelling, "Everybody's free!" It worked!

After Mrs. Dennis picked up Lauren, we played one last game. I ran around the Big House and climbed my tree. Ian and Charlie rounded the corner and stopped under a spotlight.

"Let's hide in there." Charlie pointed to the shed. Ian opened the door and looked in. I dropped to a lower branch. If I told them the shed was off limits, they'd know my hiding space. "What's in there?"

Ian reached into the shed, then straightened, hiding his arm behind his back. He whipped his arm out and pointed something at Charlie. "Give me your money!"

"Don't shoot!" Charlie raised his arms, then fell to the ground, clutching his chest, groaning, laughing. Ian stood over him, pointing a drill at his chest.

"Here I come!" Peter yelled from the other side of the Big House.

Charlie scrambled up and Ian tossed the drill back into the shed and slammed the door. They dove behind my tree. We heard footsteps. Bucky.

"Lucy?" His voice was shaking. I started down but Ian pulled Bucky behind the tree, before Peter ran by. Then I jumped.

"I fell." Bucky showed me his bloody elbow. "I wanna go home."

"Okay, I'll fix it." We walked back to the cottage. Dad, the

PT and the Ramseys were on the porch. Superior waited for me by the door.

"What happened?" Dad frowned, looking at Bucky's elbow.

"I fell," Bucky whimpered.

"I'll take care of it." I led Bucky through the porch to the kitchen. He sat on the counter and I washed his elbow. The cut wasn't very deep.

"I got caught a lot tonight," Bucky said. "Peter's cousins were too fast."

"Yeah, and you almost lost your elbow."

He giggled. "Ian hid me behind the tree."

"I know." I put on two bandages.

"Yesterday when he was at the Steeles', he got my gun out of the hedges."

I lifted my eyes. "Why was he at the Steeles'?"

Bucky jumped down. "I dunno. He was talking to Mrs. Steele."

What could he possibly have to say to her?

"I like him now," Bucky said.

"Just because he did a nice thing?"

"Two nice things," Bucky said.

Superior whined to go outside, so we both went to the yard.

Millions of stars covered the sky and the moonlight bounced off the water like tiny white Christmas tree lights.

Sometimes what seems to be one thing turns out to be another, the PT had said. Charlie's being here was better than I had imagined. And Ian was nice to Bucky. Maybe it was just me who Ian didn't like.

"Lucy!" Bucky called from the porch. Superior and I went inside. Three large drawings were spread across the table. Each showed a building. One had a pool on one side, tennis courts on the other. The second had two stories, balconies on each side. The third looked a lot like the Big House.

"John Richards came up with these options for the Big House," Dad said.

"I want the pool," Bucky said. "Then I can jump off the roof into the pool!"

"No one's going to do that." Mr. Ramsey laughed. "You picked the most expensive one. Tearing down the Big House, starting over. Yikes."

"We're going to tear down the Big House?" I asked.

"We're just talking about ideas," Dad said.

"These designs must've taken him forever," Mrs. Ramsey said.

"The guy has lots of energy," Dad said.

"Why can't we just fix it?" I asked. The PT stared at me but I didn't look at her.

"We'll try," Dad said. "No one wants to see the Big House go."

The PT was still looking at me, so I ran up the stairs. Big mouths. Big docks. A new Big House?

I pulled the box from under my bed and counted my money. If I didn't spend any of it, I'd have enough for the kayak. I put the box back and lay in the dark, listening. After the Ramseys left, Dad and the PT were quiet.

In the moonlight I saw something on my desk. The PT's rubbing alcohol.

Finally I heard her drive away. Now I could sleep.

Chapter 16

After camp on Monday I walked by Ian's house. The windows and doors were closed. Why live on the ocean if you couldn't smell or hear it?

I didn't know why I was here. Maybe Mrs. Richards would invite me in. Maybe I'd tell Mr. Richards that we had to do everything we could to keep the Big House. "Okay, Superior, let's go knock on the door." But I didn't move.

"Lucy!" Mrs. Richards walked around the corner. We stood looking at the house. "I imagine everyone thinks it's huge."

"Oh . . ." I didn't want to tell her.

"It's okay," she said. "Would you like to come in and have some iced tea? Allison went to work and Ian started sailing camp today."

I nodded and followed her through the front door. The kitchen was spread out across the back of the house. One wall was covered with framed photographs. Ian. Allison. Ian and Allison. The four of them.

"It's a bit much," Mrs. Richards said. "The double ovens. The microwaves."

"Nice pictures."

"This one is my mom. She's about twenty-five, I think. She died when I was young."

I stared at her. I didn't know anyone else who had lost her mom.

"Ian told me your mom died, too," she said. "Do you have many photos of her?"

"Some."

She poured iced tea as I got on a stool. Superior stretched out at my feet. "Do you like sugar cookies? Gingerbread?"

I didn't care about cookies. Please ask me another question about my mom, I thought. I blurted, "I was six when my mom died."

"I was twelve."

My age. We faced each other across the counter.

Mrs. Richards was serious. "Did you go to your mom's funeral?" I leaned toward her, nodding. "Oh, that's so good. So, so good."

"But I don't remember it, except the party afterward. People came over with food. I kept wandering around, watching everyone. These women were laughing."

"And you wondered, 'How can they enjoy themselves when my mom is gone?'"

121

Exactly. The women had stood against the fireplace, holding paper plates filled with tiny sandwiches. Triangles. They were smiling, until they saw me.

Mrs. Richards sighed. "At least you got to go. My father thought it was no place for children. My younger sister and I had to stay home. I was twelve! Can you imagine that? One day not long after my mom died, I came home from school and my father had packed all of my mom's things and shipped them off to her sister in Virginia." Mrs. Richards shook her head. "I never saw any of them again."

If Dad had done this, I wouldn't have the quilt Jenny had made from Mom's things. "Weren't you mad?"

"Sad, mostly. I think about her every day."

I dropped my eyes. I didn't think about my mom every day. At the same time, I had this feeling that I was *always* thinking about her.

We were quiet. But my heart raced and my skin tingled and every inch of me was awake, paying attention. "How did she die?"

"Car accident. I was in school and the principal got me out of class. I knew, before he told me, that something had happened to my mom. Isn't that odd? I just knew."

I'd known, too. But how could that be? When Mom died, I'd been at a birthday party with balloons tied to the fence and a big blue slide.

"How did your mom die?" Mrs. Richards asked.

"Glioblastoma, stage four."

She raised her eyebrows.

"It's an astrocytoma," I said. "A malignant brain tumor."

The door opened, and Allison rushed in. "Where's my cell phone?"

Mrs. Richards sat up straight. "I haven't seen it."

Allison didn't look at me as she opened and shut drawers.

"I'm going to be late for work." She turned to her mom. "Why aren't you helping me? You *never*, ever help me!"

Mrs. Richards stood, clasping her hands. "Okay, where did you have it last?"

"If I knew that, I'd know where it is!" Allison yelled.

I slid off the stool. I thought I'd better look, too.

Mr. Richards opened the door. "We were all the way there when she realized she didn't have her phone. Now I'm going to be late picking up Ian from camp."

Mrs. Richards said, "Ian's phone is still broken. He won't know what happened. And I don't want him waiting, all alone."

"I'll try the camp office." Mr. Richards flipped through his phone.

"What could *possibly* happen to him, waiting in a parking lot in the middle of nowhere?" Allison asked. "Let him figure it out! That's what you'd do if *I* was stuck there."

"Well," Mrs. Richards said. "You always seem to know what to do."

"No answer." Mr. Richards tried another number.

"You treat him like such a baby!" Allison stomped down the hall.

I stared at my iced tea. I thought maybe I should leave.

123

Allison walked back into the kitchen, smiling, and held up her phone.

"I knew you'd find it." Mrs. Richards clapped. "Where was it?"

"Under my bed," Allison said. "No clue how it got there. Probably Ian."

"Ian?" Mrs. Richards asked.

"Kidding." Allison laughed, turning to me. "Why are you here? Looking for me?"

"I invited her for iced tea," Mrs. Richards said.

"Super. You taking a break from the kiddos? Lucy, super-woman babysitter!"

Everyone laughed. Allison was president of her family.

Mr. Richards looked at Mrs. Richards. "Liz, come with us."

I started for the door. "Thanks for the iced tea."

Mrs. Richards walked me out and leaned close. "We'll finish our conversation sometime soon. Okay?" She kissed me on the cheek.

Superior and I walked down the road.

Mr. and Mrs. Richards waved as they drove past. Allison turned and stared at me through the back window. I felt something flicker in my chest, same as when you know the scary part in the movie is about to happen.

Just as they turned the corner, I waved. I should stay on her good side.

Chapter 17

On Wednesday, two days later, I dropped my bag of juice boxes on the porch. Ian sat on the swing, near the kids. Was sailing camp over already?

Mr. Richards pulled up next to the Big House in his truck. I walked over to him. "Have you found what's wrong?"

He shut his truck door. "The support beams under the porch are rotten. We're going to check and see how far back the damage goes."

I nodded. "I saw the plans you made."

"Bet I know the one *you* liked. The swimming pool! You don't think you want one and then you see the plans and think about how nice it'll be. Happens every time."

I crossed my arms. "I want the Big House to stay the way it is."

"Ah, you're one of those, huh? Nostalgic. But if we don't do something, the whole porch could cave in." He walked to the shed and opened the door. "Hey, Lucy!"

Tools were spread on the ground just inside the door.

He picked up a drill. "What's this doing on the floor? It's jammed. Were your kids here, messing with this?"

I remembered Ian pointing the drill at Charlie. "I don't think so. We were at the beach on Monday. Besides, everyone knows to stay out of the shed."

Except Ian.

Mr. Richards stared at me, face tight. "Let's make sure."

I followed him to the swing. The kids stopped talking and looked at us.

"I've been keeping my tools in the shed and I just found my drill on the floor, jammed." His voice was stern. "Does anyone know about this?"

Everyone shook their heads and said no.

Ian stared at his feet. Was he not going to say anything?

"The shed is off limits," Becca said.

"I really don't think the kids did it." I made my voice firm.

"Somebody broke it." He stared at me. "I sure didn't leave it on the shed floor."

I crossed my arms and stared back. He didn't believe me. Well, Ian was a big coward!

Mr. Richards sighed. "I'll take my tools with me. Just promise that you'll stay away from the porch area. I wouldn't want anyone to get hurt. Okay?"

"Yes!" everyone said as he walked back to the shed.

I glared at Ian. How dare he let us take the blame for this!

"Who broke it?" Lauren asked.

126

If I stared at Ian long enough, would he confess?

"Well, I didn't do it," Henry said. "Come on, I wanna play chase."

"It's hot," Becca said. "Can we go swimming?"

They all talked over each other about what they wanted to do.

"Craft, craft, craft!" Lauren and Olivia chanted.

"I don't wanna do a craft," Peter yelled. "And my mom says I don't have to stay here if I don't want to."

Everyone looked at me. I almost said, *Fine, leave!* But I didn't want him to leave, especially unhappy. "We're going to the marina to watch the boats."

Henry and Bucky cheered. Peter's face brightened. "Can Ian come?"

Everyone looked at me again. I clenched my teeth. "Fine."

The woods were cool and fragrant. The sun slanted through the treetops onto the ground and bushes and I started to relax.

If Mr. Richards had kept accusing the kids, I'd have told him what I'd seen. But it wasn't right, telling on Ian in front of everyone, especially when I wasn't completely sure.

Ian walked with his head down. Everyone was quiet.

Lauren reached for my hand. I squeezed hers. Years from now, would she remember this summer? I wanted *all* of them to remember every single thing.

As we came out of the woods at the marina, we saw a lobster boat at the dock. We ran across the parking lot and down the stairs to the water. A lobsterman pulled a lobster out of a cage, fixed rubber bands around the claws and tossed it into a barrel of water. He smiled and shot a rubber band at us. Peter grabbed it.

"I want one," Henry said. The man drew a bunch out of his pocket and threw them onto the dock. Everyone scrambled and began shooting them at each other.

"Let's see who can shoot one the farthest," Ian said.

"Wait!" I said. "Be careful!"

Becca shot her rubber band at Henry, who ducked. Peter grabbed Bucky's rubber band, but Bucky held on and when Peter pushed him, he nearly fell into the water. "Stop!" I yelled. The boys and Becca kept shooting at each other. The little girls covered their heads, shrieking. Superior paced the dock, barking at the waves.

Ian hit me in the thigh with a rubber band and I yelled, "You're making it worse!"

He shrugged. "I just want to see who can shoot the farthest."

Then Henry shot a rubber band at Lauren, who screamed, held her cheek and buried her head into my side, crying. I screamed at Ian. "You *always* cause so much trouble! Just leave!"

"I wanna Band-Aid," Lauren whimpered.

"Okay." I squeezed her shoulder and we all walked up the stairs.

Outside the marina store, I pulled back Lauren's hand.

A tiny red welt glowed on her cheek. "I'm sorry, Lauren. Nobody move. We'll be right back."

Kiki and Allison were inside.

"Hey, guys," Kiki said to us, then turned back to Allison. "Perfect! Jake'll never suspect if we do it on the night before his birthday. We'll get someone to lure him to the Big House."

Allison grinned at me, then glanced at Lauren and put her finger to her lips. I nodded, though I had no idea what they were talking about.

Lauren raised her hand to her cheek. Kiki leaned across the counter. "Oh, no, what happened?"

"She got hit with a rubber band," I said. "Can we have a Band-Aid?"

"I'll fix you up," Kiki said. "Come with me."

Lauren followed Kiki to the back room. I looked out the window at the waiting kids. Lauren's mom would be mad. I was supposed to keep everyone safe and happy.

"Who did it?" Allison started cleaning the windows.

"Ouch!" Lauren cried from the back room.

"Everyone was playing." I stood on my tiptoes, trying to see over the deli case into the back room. I sighed. "Kiki probably thinks I'm an awful camp director."

"You take that camp so seriously!" She laughed. "Listen, Kiki thinks you're awesome. We were just talking about you this morning."

"Really?" I came down from my tiptoes.

"Hey, I've got an idea," she said. "Kiki's planning a surprise birthday party for Jake. Maybe you could be the one to get him to the Big House for us."

I smiled. "Sure. I'll help!"

"Want me to talk to Kiki about it?"

"Thanks."

"Did Ian shoot the rubber band?" Allison asked.

"No. But . . ."

"But what? Did he do something else?"

"Well, I think he broke . . ." A voice in my head told me to stop because I didn't know for sure if Ian had broken the drill.

"The rope swing?" Allison waved her hand at me. "That's old news. Ian told us all about it, how you both jumped on it and the rope snapped."

"*What?*" I clenched my fists. "Ian broke that himself. I didn't do it!"

No wonder Mr. Richards didn't believe me about his drill.

Allison laughed. "Oh, don't worry. No one's mad anymore, right? And now you can enjoy a beautiful, brand-new swing. Everyone's happy."

"Ian lied!" I was so angry that I felt as if my head were going to explode. "And know what else he did? He broke your dad's drill and let me take the blame for it!"

I told her what had happened.

Allison whistled. "My dad was mad, huh?"

"He thought one of the kids did it."

"Count on Ian to make trouble." She shook her head.

Kiki and Lauren appeared. Lauren had a small bandage on her cheek, a cup of ice in her hand.

I put my arm around Lauren. "Thanks, Kiki."

"No problem."

"I was just telling Lucy how awesome her camp is," Allison said.

"I was never mature enough to run a camp like you do!" Kiki smiled at me.

Outside, Ian was gone. I made Henry apologize to Lauren; then we walked back through the woods. Only this time the light wasn't shining in such wonderful slants and the air felt humid. Ian wasn't at the Big House.

I showed Lauren's welt to Mrs. Dennis, who said, "Oh, accidents will happen."

After everyone left, Superior and I walked home.

I was still angry with Ian, but something started to not make sense. When I talked to Mr. Ramsey about the swing, he knew that Ian had broken it, not me. So maybe Ian had blamed it on me to his family and they hadn't told anyone?

Or maybe Allison had lied to me.

Chapter 18

$\sim\!\!\sim$

At lunch the next day, Bucky, Henry and Dad were talking about World War II. Back in Boston Dad and Bucky watched war shows on the History Channel for hours.

"Wouldn't it be cool if President Roosevelt was right here and we could ask him tons of questions?" Bucky sat up straight. Henry nodded, his mouth full.

Dad chuckled. "Think he'd remember everything?"

"What do you mean?" Henry asked.

"Sometimes as you get older, you remember what you *want* to remember, not necessarily how it actually happened. Your memory can play tricks on you."

But if that were true, how could you ever be sure what had *really* happened?

Dad's phone rang and he walked outside to answer. It was the PT, who was coming up again. Her friends in Portland must be sick of seeing her every weekend.

I wasn't hungry anymore. I picked up my notebook, and Superior and I walked to the dock. The sky was bright blue with batches of puffy white clouds. The air was cool and breezy and the dock rocked in the current.

I wanted to use my imagination to draw. I closed my eyes. The seals: I saw their shiny coats, how their heads connected to their bodies with thick black necks. I opened my eyes and drew. I looked up when I heard voices.

Ian and Mrs. Steele stood on the Steeles' dock. Ian lifted the tarp on the kayak and squatted. Then Mrs. Steele turned, cupped her hands to her mouth and called, "Lucy! Come here!"

Superior and I walked over to their dock.

"Hello, you two," Mrs. Steele said. "Ian's here to look at the kayak."

She smiled at him but he kept his eyes lowered.

"His dad told him that he must learn everything he can about kayaks before they buy one of their own. Why don't you two take it out?"

We both looked at Mrs. Steele.

"Go on, go ahead," she said. "The old girl hasn't been out all season."

No way would I go out there with him. But I didn't want him taking it out alone. He might wreck it. Or worse, he might like it. Then he'd be here every day.

"Helen!" Mr. Steele stood at the top of the stairs. "I need your help!"

"Oh, honestly." Mrs. Steele sighed. "You two can figure this out. It's easy."

Ian pulled paddles and life jackets from under the upside-down kayak. When Superior sniffed the life jackets, he smiled at her.

I squatted next to her. I was still angry with Ian but I felt a little guilty, too. Had Allison told Ian or their dad what I'd said about the drill? Ian didn't seem angry.

But why should I apologize when he'd never apologized to me?

Small ripples bounced against the dock, rocking it gently, as a sailboat motored into the bay. Superior walked to the edge of the wood, ears pricked.

"You're really lucky to have such a cool dog."

"I know. Thanks," I said. "I thought you were going to sailing camp."

"I went for a couple days. Sailing's kinda boring. I wanna try this." He stood. "Help me."

We flipped the kayak over. It was a two-person ocean kayak, which meant you didn't sit in a cockpit but on top. These kayaks didn't tip as easily as regular kayaks, but they were still dangerous, especially if you'd never been on one.

Ian put on a life jacket and zipped it to his chin. "Are you gonna go out with me?"

I glanced at Superior. "I don't want to leave her on the dock."

"She can come with us. There's room. She can sit in the middle."

"She'll just bark at the waves. Which might tip us."

"Whatever."

We carried the kayak to the edge of the dock and set it in the water. I held the bow while he climbed on top, then gave him a push. The kayak tipped side to side, but he steadied it as he paddled away.

He'd need help lifting the kayak when he returned, so I waited.

Twenty minutes later I saw him, his strokes even and strong, the kayak steadier. He looked comfortable, gliding on the water.

"This is so cool!" He paddled up to the dock and I leaned over and held the bow. "But I can't go very fast. It'd be better with two people. How do you turn?"

We lifted the kayak onto the dock.

"I don't know," I said. "I've never, well, I've never gone kayaking."

"You've been coming here your whole life! What, you're afraid of the water?" He laughed, unzipped his jacket and tossed it on the dock.

He knew! Or was he joking? We covered the kayak, then climbed the stairs.

"How was it?" Mrs. Steele called from their porch.

"Great! Thank you so much. Can I use it again?" Ian grinned.

"Sure," Mr. Steele said. "Anytime!"

"Bye." Ian grinned again, then disappeared around the side of the cottage.

I stomped back to my yard and dropped into my wagon under the birch tree. Ian had taken out the Steeles' kayak. Big deal. What was wrong with me?

I glanced down at the bay, which was still and blue. Kayaking must feel as if you were sitting right on the water. So close that you could touch it with your fingers. So close that you felt like *part* of the water.

I remembered Mom smiling on the dock, hand shading the sun. She'd loved the water. Had she liked kayaking? I wished I knew.

Mrs. Richards had been in school when she'd gotten the news about her mom. She'd been where she was supposed to be, doing what she was supposed to be doing. I'd been at a party, which I'd wanted to go to more than anything. I sighed.

Dad walked around the corner and sat in the grass next to me. We hardly talked about the day Mom died. How it had happened. How he had told me. Probably because it was so sad.

Had he been there when I'd gone down the slide? Who pulled me out of the water?

"Remember the birthday party I went to the day Mom died?" I glanced at Dad but he seemed okay, so I kept going. "I was just thinking about that slide at their pool."

Dad frowned. "The Rechts? They didn't have a slide."

I jerked my head to look at him. "But I remember one, a big blue slide."

"No, I'm sure. Mom and I'd been at that pool many times."
I reached for Superior.

"Maybe you're thinking of the Reecers' pool. They hosted a party the year I coached your soccer team. They had a big slide. You girls were pretty intimidated by it."

"Oh."

"You okay?" he asked.

"Sure." I started to get up.

Dad grabbed my arm. "Is camp okay?"

I nodded.

"Good. You know, well . . . I know we don't always talk about things . . . I count on you, Goose. You've always been so darn capable. But Julia wonders if you might be . . ."

I bolted from the yard.

Chapter 19

~~~

Superior and I were out before breakfast, wandering along the narrow shore underneath the stairs to the dock. We found a dead jellyfish the size of my hand. Mei sure would have loved to see this.

The day before, she'd emailed. Earlier I'd written, saying that I wished we could stay at Taylor the next year, and this was what she said: *Me 2. But we'll be 2gether, right? Maybe we'll be on the same team!!! Even if we're not, we'll sit 2gether at lunch!*

That made me smile.

Then she wrote *Guess who I saw at Star Market? Mrs. Jonas! She wanted 2 know if U are drawing. I said, YES!!! U should write her coz she wants to hear from U!*

Mrs. Jonas? Once I left Taylor, I thought I'd never talk to her again. I'd write soon, maybe even send her a drawing.

I climbed onto the dock and opened my notebook. I'd made lots of drawings. Fish, mallards, geese, boats, docks, an eagle. Back in Boston I looked through this book every night before bed. The place I loved most was the last thing I saw before I slept.

"Lucy!" Bucky stood at the top of the stairs. "Dad says we have to clean."

I closed my notebook and started up the stairs.

"You're up early." Dad was at the kitchen table, spreading peanut butter on toast. I nodded and poured a bowl of cereal. "Julia will be here in a little while."

"Can we take her camping on Upper Egg?" Bucky asked.

Dad glanced at me. "Sometime, Buck. The weather looks too iffy for tomorrow."

"Can we at least show her Pear?" Bucky asked. Dad nodded.

"We're not going to Pear," I said.

"Why not?" Bucky asked.

"She doesn't want to see it."

"How d'you know?"

"Because she doesn't need to see every little thing we do!" I yelled, then put my elbows on the table and sank my head into my hands.

"Lucy." Dad's voice was so soft that I looked at him. Bucky looked, too. "Julia's kind and generous and smart. And, well, I'm in love with her. She loves me, too."

Why couldn't he just be happy with things as they were?

"This doesn't mean that I don't still love Mom," he said. "I'll always love her."

"You love both of them." Bucky said this as if it made perfect sense.

I glared at him, then reached under the table for Superior.

"I want to tell you about her," Dad said. "How she grew up. When she married."

I held up my hand. "I don't want to hear about it."

"Are you going to get married?" Bucky asked, milk dripping from his mouth.

I took a napkin across his chin, then wiped up the milk on the table.

Dad looked at me, then Bucky. "What do you think about that? About her living with us?"

"She'll be our new mom," Bucky said.

"Stepmom," I said.

Dad nodded. "A stepmom. Right. You don't seem to like that too much, Goose."

I glanced at the clock. "Come on, Buck, let's get this over with."

On the porch I piled newspapers, swept the floor, dusted the tables. When I ran out of things to clean, I rearranged the pillows. Dad came up behind me and I turned and put my head to his chest, tears burning my eyes.

He hugged me. "Oh, Goose, you were so sad when Mom died."

But *he* was the one who'd been so sad.

"I don't like her." I pushed away. The PT hadn't really done anything wrong. And she was funny talking about Harry Hen and Ian and Charlie spying. But if I told Dad, he'd think it was okay to marry her.

"Okay," Dad said finally.

The PT drove up to the cottage. I saw how Dad's happy look faded—*The talk didn't go well,* I imagined him saying— but when I glanced back at the PT, she was smiling.

We decided to go to Pear. We made sandwiches and packed the cooler. We were headed to the stairs when Ian walked across the Steeles' yard, his long arms swinging.

"I was gonna take out the kayak," he said. "Are you going to Pear?"

"Want to come?" Dad glanced at me and I shrugged. He motioned toward the PT.

"Oh," I said. "This is, um, Julia."

Ian thrust out his hand. "Ian Richards. Nice to meet you, Julia."

"Nice to meet you." She shook his hand, smiling.

Great. He was going to suck up to her, too.

Ian called his parents and then we were on our way. Bucky and the PT sat up front, laughing as Superior barked and snapped at the spray. Ian stood next to Dad, and I sat behind the windshield, my life jacket zipped to my chin, my hands gripping the seat.

Halfway to Pear, Dad slowed. The water was calm, the bay fairly empty of boats.

"The shipwreck!" Bucky jumped up and dug both face masks out of the bench. He handed one to Ian, whose eyes widened.

"Don't exaggerate, Buck. It's not really a shipwreck," I said.

"Yeah, it is." Bucky turned to Ian. "When Dad was a kid,

141

this big sailboat sank during a storm. If the water's clear, you can see it. It's so cool!"

I glanced over the side. The water was dark and murky, full of hidden rocks and steep drops. One time, years earlier, I jumped in with Dad and looked down at the sailboat. It was both beautiful and scary how the seaweed wound around the rusty mast.

Ian adjusted his mask and glanced at me. "You don't want to go?"

"Nah." I shrugged, as if to say that I'd seen it a hundred times.

He and Bucky jumped. Superior ran from one end of the boat to the other, barking. I glanced at the PT.

"You don't like the water much, do you?" she said.

"It's okay. I just don't feel like swimming today."

Bucky and Ian wore life jackets, although Ian hardly needed one. He looked natural as he kicked, then floated on his back. They found the sailboat and called to us. The PT watched as if it were the most fascinating thing she'd ever seen.

Then Dad tossed them an inner tube and rope and we dragged them to shore on Pear Island. We anchored, left the cooler and blankets on the beach and started up the path. The air was cool and sweet and the bushes left dew on our shorts and legs.

Dad told Ian about the eagle nest and now Ian had a million questions. How big did nests get? How big were the eagles? Could we see the nest on our way back?

"It's tough to navigate the waters there," Dad said. "Too many rocks."

I brought up the rear. As we neared the top, the PT turned and whispered, "He sure talks a lot."

I couldn't help smiling.

We reached the grassy opening. The sun was hot, the wind warm. The PT walked to the edge and looked out. Superior trotted next to her and started digging. Bucky chased a toad back down the path. Dad and Ian were finally quiet.

I walked to the PT and pointed across the bay. "That's Pierson Point."

"It's so beautiful." She took a deep breath. "I like this island, too."

"Those are wild blueberry bushes down there," I said.

She started down the slope and I followed. The bushes were full of tiny dark blue berries. She pulled a branch toward her face. "Can you eat them?"

"They're a little sour still."

She popped one into her mouth and sucked in her cheeks. "Sour, yes!"

I glanced up the hill toward Ian, who talked with Dad.

"He's a character." She laughed quietly. "Impulsive yet endearing. But I wonder if he's overcompensating. Covering up for something."

"What?"

"Oh, I don't know. There's always the other side of you, right?"

"Let's go!" Bucky yelled. "I'm starving!"

We hiked down to the shore and ate. Then we headed back across the bay. The water was choppier, and the wind strong, so Dad drove slowly. I sat in my seat, holding on. Ian leaned over the side, dragging his arm in the water.

The other side of you. I loved the water but I was also afraid of it. Mei was shy but not with me. Was this what the PT meant?

At our dock, I jumped out and tied up the boat. Then Bucky ran to Henry's and Dad and the PT went for a walk.

"Well, I'll see you," Ian said. "Thanks."

"Bye."

He walked to the Steeles' cottage and knocked. Mrs. Steele answered, waved to me, then stepped aside as Ian walked in.

What?

I imagined him at their table, Mr. Steele reading the paper and Mrs. Steele taking muffins out of the oven. I knew they loved me. But what if they liked Ian better than me?

I was being ridiculous. The Steeles had known me since I was born.

Finally Ian went into their shed, got a rake and cleaned up leaves and dead grass.

Superior and I walked over. "What are you doing?"

He kept raking. "In exchange for using the kayak, I'm doing stuff."

I grabbed a rake. It didn't take long to dump everything in the woods. As we put the rakes back in the shed, Ian said,

"You helped, so now you gotta go out in the kayak with me tomorrow."

I hesitated. "Okay."

"You'll like it." He grinned and walked away.

I reached for Superior. What had I done?

Chapter 20

The next day Ian and I stood on the Steeles' dock, wearing life jackets. We flipped the kayak and set it on the water. Ian lowered himself onto it and squinted up at me as I chewed the inside of my cheek.

"We'll be able to go faster with two people," he said. "It's not that hard. You just have to balance."

"I'll watch." I took off my life jacket and dropped it but in my head I screamed at myself, *Go!*

"You *are* afraid of the water. I knew it!" He laughed and threw back his head, then pushed away from the dock and paddled toward the marina.

He'll have to figure out how to get the kayak onto the dock by himself! I thought. I stomped up the stairs, Superior close behind.

"Hello!" Mrs. Steele called from her porch. "I thought you'd be out with Ian."

"No. Need anything done around the yard?"

"Between you and Ian we'll have the cleanest yard on the Point. No, we're fine today. Thanks for asking. Come in!"

I walked in and sat facing the yard. We talked about how quickly the wild blueberries were ripening and how Superior's white hair made her look "distinguished." The whole time I was bouncing my knee, irritated.

Then the PT drove up to our cottage. The night before, she'd left here at midnight to go to her friend's house in Portland. Dad walked out and hugged her.

"What do you think of Julia?" Mrs. Steele asked. I glanced at my watch. Ian had left a half hour earlier. Did he stop at the marina?

"She's okay." They stared at me, waiting. "She's tall."

"She has a lot of teeth." Mr. Steele smiled at me.

"Walter!" Mrs. Steele said. We laughed.

Mrs. Steele brought out a plate of blueberry scones and I ate two, slipping half of the second to Superior. Then I thanked them and left. At the edge of the yard, I looked down. Ian, just a speck in the water, paddled toward me.

Superior and I took the path to the Big House. A Dumpster sat off to the side, empty. I ran back to the cottage. Dad and the PT were on the porch.

"There's a Dumpster at the Big House," I said through the screen.

"Really?" Dad asked.

"Does this mean they're going to tear it down?" I asked.

"That's a pretty big leap. Everyone would have to agree. I'll talk to Joel tonight."

We were going to the Ramseys' for a cookout. I walked past Bucky and Henry, who were playing with army men in the yard, and looked down at the Steeles' dock. The kayak was in the water, tied to a post. That wasn't very responsible of Ian.

"I need your help," I said to Bucky and Henry. Down on the dock we lifted the kayak and flipped it, then slid the paddles and life jackets underneath.

I knew from my magazine that sit-on-top kayaks were pretty safe. If you tipped, you couldn't get trapped inside, as in a regular kayak, so you didn't have to practice rolls or sliding out of the kayak underwater.

I pulled the tarp over the kayak.

Later I sat at the edge of the Ramseys' lawn, near the stairs that led to their dock. It was nearly dusk and the water below was still and gray. Jake Ramsey and two of his friends did cannonballs off the dock. Earlier Dad had asked me to watch Bucky after dinner so the adults could talk. Bucky and Henry walked on the rocks under the dock.

I glanced at the adults. Mr. Ramsey had said that he didn't know why the Dumpster was at the Big House and that nothing had been decided. Then he and Dad started talking about the Red Sox.

The PT walked toward me. I pulled Superior close.

"I haven't really talked to you since Pear Island." She sat, her back to the water. "You and Ian had fun?"

I nodded. I wanted to talk about him but I didn't know what to say. I watched Bucky and Henry climb onto the Ramseys' dock.

The PT took her palm back and forth over the top of the grass. Her brown hair fell over her shoulders, and her white skin was red with sunburn. Maybe she'd realize that the sun wasn't good for her. Maybe she wouldn't want to spend summers up here.

Superior sniffed her sandal.

"Has she always been your dog?" the PT asked. I nodded. "That's nice, huh?"

Was she going to start asking a million questions again?

"How is camp?"

"Fine." My voice was sharp. She sat back. Superior pricked her ears, then trotted over to a flower bed.

The PT leaned in. "Listen, Lucy, I want you to know—"

"Superior!" I ran to her. She'd started digging, dirt and flowers flying. When I pulled on her collar, she sat, her nose caked with dirt. I picked up a flower, its stem broken. "Oh, no."

The PT walked over. "We might be able to save a few of these. I'll go find a trowel and be right back." She walked up to the Ramseys' cottage.

I stood there, staring at the flowers. What did the PT want to tell me? I turned and ran for our cottage.

I gave Superior water and brushed her. Then I sat at my puzzle.

But after fifteen minutes I started feeling guilty about the flower bed and leaving the PT and not thanking the Ramseys for dinner, so I walked back. The PT was on the porch with the others. The flower bed had been raked, only a few flowers replanted.

I walked to the top of the Ramseys' stairs and looked down. Henry stood at the end of the dock, watching the older boys swim to the buoy. Where was Bucky?

Then I saw him in the water, halfway to the buoy. I ran down the stairs.

"Bucky, come back!" I screamed. The older boys were nearly at the buoy, way out in the bay. Bucky kept stopping and treading water before swimming again. His strokes were quick and jerky. He was tiring. It was too far for him.

I kicked off my flip-flops and dove into the water. The cold slapped me in the face, then shot down my body. Seaweed skimmed my hands and legs, but I just kept putting one arm over the other. Bucky waited, head bobbing against the open water.

"Are you okay?"

"I thought I could do it." He cried, gulping breaths.

I treaded water. "Just go on your side. I'll swim back next to you."

We faced each other, swimming sidestroke. Superior barked at us from the dock. Bucky whimpered, "It's too far. I'm too tired." But I kept telling him, "Breathe. Swim."

Dad, the PT and the Ramseys were waiting on the dock. I climbed out, followed by Bucky. Dad handed me a towel, then wrapped another around Bucky, who shivered, staring at his feet. Goose bumps broke out all over my body.

"You know you're not supposed to swim out there on your own, *ever*," Dad said.

"But I thought I could make it." Bucky dropped his eyes and sniffled with tears.

"Jake should've known Bucky was coming after him," Mrs. Ramsey said.

"This isn't Jake's fault." Dad turned to me. "Where were *you*? I asked you to watch him."

I frowned. This was Bucky's fault. "I just went back to the cottage for a minute."

"And that's what you call watching him?"

"Well, Bucky never listens to me, anyway!"

"I don't?" Bucky said.

I glared at him. Then my shoulders sank, because Dad was right. I *had* been responsible for Bucky. I shivered—the night air was cool—and licked the salt off my lips.

Dad sighed. "Okay, Lucy, you and Buck head back. We'll be along soon."

"Thanks for dinner," I said to Mr. and Mrs. Ramsey. "Sorry about the flowers."

"No harm done," Mrs. Ramsey said. I started for the cottage, Bucky trailing me.

"Will you turn on the shower?" he asked.

"Sure." I walked around the cottage to the outdoor shower.

Bucky jumped into the hot stream of water. "Thanks. And I *do* listen to you!"

"Whatever."

Inside, I took a shower while Superior waited on the

151

bathroom rug. She knew something was wrong—she kept bumping into me—and finally I bent over and hugged her. "It's okay, Superior. It's not your fault."

I didn't look at Bucky as we passed each other in the hallway.

Dad waited at the bottom of the stairs. "I'm sorry I was so angry, Goose. You always watch Bucky. I know you take a lot of responsibility for him."

I nodded.

"I got scared," he said. "Buck's an okay swimmer, but it was a long way out there. Listen, if you watch him and want to do something else, tell me. And you were brave to go after him. I know you don't like the water."

I felt myself soften. "Okay. And I'm sorry I left."

Dad nodded, then climbed the stairs. I walked onto the porch. The PT was reading on the couch and didn't look up when I sat at my puzzle. I picked up a blue ocean piece. Or was it the sky? I turned it over in my hand.

The ocean was cold. I couldn't remember the last time I'd swum that far. But I was fine. I glanced at the PT. If she hadn't been here, then Dad wouldn't have asked me to watch Bucky and I wouldn't have left the Ramseys'. It was her fault.

June bugs bounced off the screens. A cool breeze blew onto the porch and I heard the faint clanging of the buoys in the bay. Then I saw a fit in my puzzle. How easy! Why hadn't I seen that before?

"Yes!" I glanced at the PT again, daring her to look at me.

Then I'd jerk my head away from her. She licked her finger and turned a page in her book, her head down.

My stomach sank. People were responsible for each other, and that night I'd been responsible for Bucky. I could blame her all I wanted, but it wasn't her fault.

If I met her somewhere, like at a grocery store, and she had nothing to do with Dad, then I'd probably like her. I should apologize for running away and leaving her with the flowers, but then she might think it was okay to be here. Still, I should say *something*.

"Did you know that the Nile River is 4,132 miles long?" I remembered how amazed Lauren and I had been when Allison had rattled off those facts about raccoons.

She raised her eyebrows but didn't smile. "Yes, it's the longest river in the world." Then she went back to her book. Okay, she was mad at me.

"Thanks for the rubbing alcohol," I said. My ears had started to feel better.

Finally she glanced at me, her eyes soft, big mouth turned down. Maybe she wasn't angry, but disappointed. Hot prickles started up my neck.

Dad came to the doorway, smiling at her—a different smile than he gave me. Excited. So, so happy. The prickles crept up to my cheeks and now I knew what they were. *Guilt.* Because I was mean to her or because of something else?

I jumped up. I couldn't stand these feelings anymore.

Chapter 21

"Enemy ahead, six o'clock!" Bucky, in his camouflage pajamas, ran into the yard. Henry followed, wearing an old army jacket that hung to his knees. They used sticks as guns and pinecones as grenades.

I watched from the porch, then pulled money out of my pocket. Another week of camp ended that day. I was two hundred dollars away from my goal. I'd make it as long as I didn't spend a cent.

When Dad came to the doorway, I swept my money into my lap. A twenty-dollar bill fell onto Superior, who was stretched out across my feet. She sniffed it, then laid her head back down.

"I don't know about you"—Dad pointed to the boys, then sat next to me—"but I feel a whole lot better knowing the cottage is fully protected."

I smiled and shoved the bills back into my pocket. I felt

lucky to have a dad who was president of our family and who hadn't packed up Mom's things and shipped them off to Michigan after she died. He picked up a puzzle piece.

"Not this again." I took the piece from him and we laughed.

"I'd hoped we could camp on Upper Egg this weekend, but the weather might not cooperate again." His voice was so serious that I squeezed my puzzle piece. "And Julia has to work this weekend, so she won't be up."

I stared down, trying to hide a smile.

"Can we please talk about her?"

"I don't have anything to say."

"You know, she was married once. She lost her husband."

I stood. Why did he want to talk about things all the time now?

"Will someone help me?" Bucky called. "I can't reach my gun."

I ran out the door and pulled Bucky's stick from high in the hedges.

When I heard something behind me, I turned to see Ian pushing a wheelbarrow full of compost in the Steeles' backyard. I walked over.

"I'm spreading this stuff in the garden, then taking out the kayak." He tipped the wheelbarrow. "Man, how can something that smells so bad be so good?"

He held his nose and shuddered, his arms flopping. I laughed, then picked up the rake and started spreading the compost. Ian pulled out weeds. We finished in a half hour and Mrs. Steele handed us each a blueberry muffin.

"Wow!" Ian smiled. "Your garden is the nicest one I've ever seen."

Suck-up!

"Thank you, Ian. And thanks, you two, for your hard work."

"Sure." Ian bit into his muffin. "Good!"

I glanced at Mrs. Steele. So far only the PT didn't seem snowed by Ian.

"You're both welcome to the kayak," she said. "Go on. Enjoy."

Superior and I followed Ian to the dock. He handed me a life jacket and I zipped it to my chin. The water was calm but I saw how it stirred underneath the surface. Her nose over the edge of the dock, Superior paced, smelling, watching.

"Are you coming?" Ian said as we lowered the kayak.

"What about Superior?"

"She can come with us." He sighed. "You're afraid of drowning, aren't you?"

I looked at the water, then nodded.

"You know, only, like, nine people drown in the U.S. every day," he said.

That made 63 per week and 252 per month. "How'd you know that?"

"I found it on a Web site during our science project." He smiled and I smiled back. We climbed onto the kayak and pushed off. Superior started barking at us.

"We're not going far," I yelled to her. The kayak wobbled and our paddles collided in the air until we coordinated our strokes. Then we glided.

My heart pounded and everything came at me at once. The cold water, the warm salt air, the bold blue sky. I looked straight ahead at Bucket Island, with its evergreens and birch trees. I reached over and skimmed my hand on top of the water.

But Superior wouldn't stop barking, so we turned back. We watched her pace, her neck stretched so far that it looked as if it could snap.

"We're coming!" When we were only thirty feet away, she jumped, crashing into the water, and swam toward us, her black and white snout just above the surface.

Everything happened fast. Superior tried to climb onto the kayak, her nails scraping and sliding. I panicked and leaned toward her, and we tipped. I went headfirst into the water, the shocking cold freezing my face, my breath. But I bobbed to the surface. Ian was in the water, too. The kayak floated upside down beside us.

"Let's get Superior to the dock," he said. We swam on either side of her. It had been a long time since she'd swum this far.

"Come on, you can do it," I said.

In a few minutes we reached the dock. I tried coaxing Superior up the ladder but she wouldn't go. Ian climbed up; then I did and she followed. On the dock she shook and water flew everywhere. She sat and looked at me, panting heavily. I kissed her wet nose.

Ian jumped back in after the kayak and paddles. Superior and I climbed onto the rocks and sand. I waded into the water and helped him flip the kayak and lift it out.

"That was wild!" Ian collapsed onto the dock, laughing. "You go much faster with two people paddling! Next time we'll take it around the Point."

I wrung out the bottom of my shirt and pulled my wet shorts away from me. I curtsied and Ian cracked up.

Twice in one week I'd gone into the water and nothing bad had happened. If I hadn't reached for Superior, we wouldn't have tipped. Maybe we *could* go around the Point. I'd done it!

"We went flying into the water!" Ian kept laughing. "That was so much fun."

I grinned. Then we sat in the sun, quiet. Ian lay on his back, his arms and legs spread, his eyes closed. The year before, Annie had put him on her list of the top five cutest boys in our class. Kendra Willet said she held hands with him at the movies.

But I knew that at any moment, he could do something jerky. Maybe break something. People didn't just *change* all of a sudden.

I looked at his freckles and long fingers and the way his chin pushed out. He was kind of cute, I guessed, as long as he was just lying there. I could tell I was blushing. I stretched out next to him and let the sun dry me.

158

After a while Dad called to us, and Ian followed me onto our porch. We told Dad about the kayak.

"Then Superior jumped into the water and tried to get up and we tipped over." Ian laughed. "It was so cool!"

"Your first wet exit." Dad grinned. "Did you like kayaking?"

"Yes. Except I was worried about Superior."

"Take her with you next time," Dad said. I nodded.

"You should see Superior swim," Ian said. "She's so strong. And she follows Lucy everywhere. I wish I had a dog like her."

"We're lucky," Dad said.

Ian smiled, then looked around the porch. Our cottage was different from his house. What did he think about the water stains on the ceiling? The mildew smell?

What did he think about *me*?

"Well, I should go," he said. "See you!"

I watched as he opened the porch door, then walked onto the road.

"Seems like you two have finally become friends," Dad said.

"We went kayaking, that's all." My cheeks were hot, so I hurried across the porch and climbed the stairs to my room.

My shorts and shirt were dry but inside my pocket the money was still damp. I took out the bills and spread them across my desk. Next time I'd wear my bathing suit.

I jerked my head up. Next time!

Were we friends now?

Chapter 22

Lauren and Stevie were in their suits when I arrived to babysit, so we walked down to the water. The tide was low and they waded out, looking for shells. I kept glancing at Ian's house but it was closed up tight.

I'd brought my notebook and bird book, but Lauren didn't want to draw.

"Let's play house," she said. We draped towels over the railing on their dock, making a house. Lauren and I sat underneath while Stevie filled a bucket, brought it to us and dumped it out on the dock. Water, sand and rocks spewed across the wood.

"Dinner!" he said.

We pretended to eat, gushing over how good it was. He giggled, waddled back down the dock and filled his bucket. We did this over and over.

The air was hot, humid and still. We were sweating as the

sun forced its way through tiny holes in the towels. I faced the Debacle so I could see if anyone went in or out. "Can't we do something else?"

"No!" they both said. Stevie waddled up and dumped the bucket.

Lauren pretended to eat. "These pork chops are scrump delicious."

I laughed. The game was real to them.

When I finished babysitting, I walked past Mrs. Richards, who was opening her car door. "Hi."

She smiled. "Hello, Lucy. Superior."

I suddenly had so many questions that I didn't know where to start. "Can I ask you something?" She nodded. "Did you have a stepmom?"

Her cloudy eyes widened. "My dad remarried sixteen months after my mom died. She and my dad are still married, although I don't have much of a relationship with her."

"Why not?"

"Oh, it's complicated." I waited and she sighed. "Let's see. She's . . . distant. Hard to know."

"Like how?"

"The week after they married, she sent me off to sleepaway camp for the summer. And I can't remember her asking me one question or coming to many of my school events. She just wanted my dad, not us."

"Oh." Dad would never let the PT send us off somewhere.

"Why are you asking? Will you have a stepmom soon?"

"Maybe."

"I've heard plenty of stories about wonderful stepmoms," she said. "I think my situation was unusual. What's this woman like?"

I scratched Superior behind her ears. "She's tall."

Mrs. Richards smiled. "It's pretty normal not to like your dad's girlfriend, especially if you know she's about to become his wife."

Really? Maybe hundreds, maybe even thousands, of people didn't like their dads' girlfriends. I wasn't alone.

Ian walked out the door, a duffel bag over his shoulder.

"I'm taking Ian back home for the week, to lacrosse camp," she said.

"Oh." I felt a little sting in my chest. The week? "No kayaking."

But he was silent.

Mrs. Richards opened her car door. "Nice to see you again."

"Bye." I waved as they drove away.

Halfway to our cottage I realized that I didn't have my books, so Superior and I went back to the Dennises'. As I walked between the Debacle and Dennises', I saw Allison and the older girls on the Debacle's dock. The Pollards' boat was tied to a post.

I picked up my books, then stood on the shore and watched. The girls were laughing as they talked over each other.

Tonya waved to me. "Hey, Lucy, come here!"

On the dock, Danielle and Tonya stuck out their arms.

"Who has the better tan?" Tonya asked. "Allison and Kiki split the vote."

"We have way more important things to talk about than tans," Kiki said.

"Shush!" Danielle said. "Okay, Lucy, say it. *I* have the better tan."

I stared at Danielle's arm, then Tonya's. I couldn't tell the difference. Plus if I said one was tanner, the other might get mad. "I think Superior has the best tan."

Everyone laughed. Kiki put her arm around me and said, "That's just perfect, Lucy." Then they plopped down on beach towels spread on the dock.

I nudged Superior and she sat. I leaned against the railing, watching.

"It doesn't matter." Tonya sighed. "Because the Big House lights are so bad that on the night of the party, we'll all look tan."

"Now, now, no dissing the Big House," Kiki said. "Did I tell you that Mrs. Ramsey invited a couple of Jake's college friends?"

"About twenty times," Allison said.

Jake's surprise party. I glanced at Allison but her eyes were closed, her face tilted toward the sun.

They went over the plan: Allison was in charge of music, Kiki the decorations, and Tonya and Danielle were picking up the food. What about my part? When they started talking about the marina, I shot a look at Allison again.

She watched Kiki, not looking at me.

And then I realized that Allison hadn't said a word to them about me.

Why? Had she planned all along not to?

I felt a little sick. "I gotta go."

Later that night, as I lay in bed, I wanted to think about my conversation with Mrs. Richards. But all I kept seeing was Allison's face, turned away from me.

And now I worried. Had she told anyone that I'd said Ian had broken the drill?

Chapter 23

On Wednesday the kids and I built a huge mud castle at the beach.

"Where's Ian?" Peter tossed his football, then caught it.

"He went back to Boston," I said. He'd been gone nearly a week and the Point was quiet without him. I'd gone over to the Steeles' dock, but didn't have the nerve to take the kayak out on my own.

"If he was here, we'd play football," Peter whined.

I rubbed my sandy hands together. "I'm done with this. I'll play."

We threw his ball back and forth a few times. When Becca tried to join, Peter wouldn't throw to her, so she stomped off. I brought her back just as Peter threw the football into the castle, wrecking it. Everyone yelled at him and Olivia cried all the way back to the Big House.

We'd run out of water bottles again, so the kids drank from

the hose. Bucky made a puddle in the grass and dirt off to the side of the Big House, near the garden. Then Lauren dropped Poley into it and burst into tears.

I ran around the Big House and into the kitchen to search for paper towels. When I got back outside, I gasped. The kids were sliding in the puddle, clumps of grass pulled up, mud everywhere.

"Stop!" I grabbed the hose from Bucky. Mud and water dripped from them. Olivia's pink tank top had turned brown. Mud was piled on Bucky's head. The flowers in the garden were speckled.

"Your moms are gonna be mad!" I glanced at my watch: 11:45! I hosed them off, but Olivia's shirt was still brown. Becca picked mud from her ears.

Mrs. Avery pulled up to the Big House. She wore makeup and a dress and she was frowning. "What's this? Olivia, your new tank top."

"I'm sorry." I cringed. "I went inside for a minute and when I came back . . ."

"We're headed to Portland." She sighed. "We'll go to the cottage to change."

She handed me money and I thanked her, still cringing. Peter and Becca ran off when their mom drove up. Mrs. Dennis just smiled and didn't seem to care. I was trying to push the grass clumps back into place when Mr. Ramsey walked by.

"What happened?"

"We drank from the hose because I ran out of water and I had to go inside and I shouldn't have left, but Poley was wet and I couldn't find the paper towels. I'm sorry."

The puddle glistened in the sun. Mr. Ramsey pulled up a clump. "We may need to reseed. We want to save this part of the yard when the porch comes down. I think it'd be a good idea not to have the hose out again."

I nodded. "Okay."

"Everything else okay?"

"Yes, we weren't even inside today."

"I'm taking the boys tubing. Want to come?"

"Thanks, but I can't," I said. Mr. Ramsey nodded, then disappeared down the path with the boys. Superior and I headed back to the cottage and down to the dock.

Instead of water bottles, I'd buy paper cups, which were cheaper, and we'd use the faucet inside the Big House kitchen. We also needed more snacks. Maybe grass seed, too.

It all sounded expensive.

"Goose, want some lunch?" Dad started down the stairs. I was about to cry, so I kept my eyes on the dock. He stood over me. "What's the matter?"

Then it all spilled out of me: the hose, the grass seed, the supplies.

"I'll drive you to the supermarket," Dad said. "And we'll take a look at the lawn. If we need to reseed, we will. It shouldn't be too hard. Okay?"

I nodded but I still saw Lauren's face, streaked with tears, and Peter's frown because he wanted Ian. "I'm not doing a very good job."

"What?" He sat.

I shook my head and started to cry. "The kids aren't very happy!"

"Whoa. You think it's your responsibility to make them *happy?*"

"It's my camp, my job."

"No, Goose. You can work at trying to make camp fun. But how people feel and what happens to them are *their* responsibilities."

This didn't make sense. Dad always liked the drawings I showed him. The eagles made him excited. His whole body smiled when he saw the PT. You *could* change people's feelings. You *could* make them happy or sad.

Mr. Ramsey drove by in his speedboat and Bucky and Henry waved from the inner tube. We waved back. Dad scratched Superior behind her ears.

More than anything, I wanted the kids to be happy. I wanted them to have great memories of camp, that summer, the Point. So they'd never, ever forget.

"You okay?"

I nodded. Dad pulled me up and we walked to the cottage.

Later I bought cups and snacks to last one more week, grass seed and fertilizer. When I looked at my receipts, I was pretty sure that I wouldn't have enough money for the kayak.

We decided to go to the Clam Shack for dinner. Halfway there Dad's phone rang. "That's terrific! Okay. I'll call later."

He put his phone away. "Julia's coming on Friday. She got off work."

"We could go camping!" Bucky said. "And look for the giant horseshoe crabs again. Remember, Lucy, last time we were there? I bet Julia'd like to see one."

"She doesn't care about crabs, Bucky."

"How do you know?"

"Because I just do!" I yelled.

Dad turned to look at me. Bucky slunk back into his seat.

"Lucy, I love her and she loves me and I want her to be here with us," Dad said. "You certainly don't. I don't know what to do anymore!"

I didn't know, either.

"Mom would've wanted this for us, I know it." Dad's voice was softer.

It was normal not to like your dad's girlfriend. But that day this didn't make me feel better. "At least can Jenny stay with us at home?"

"Jenny's leaving?" Bucky bolted upright.

"No one's talking about Jenny leaving," Dad said.

At the Clam Shack Bucky ate a hot dog. Dad and I picked at the fried clams, not eating much. Dad sat hunched over his plate, quiet. I wanted to say something to make him happy, but what?

It was dark by the time we reached the dirt road to the Point.

I felt the ocean on my skin, in my lungs, even if I couldn't see it.

I glanced at Dad, his face lit up by the dashboard. He'd told me that what people feel is their own responsibility. But wasn't I responsible for his being unhappy right now?

Dad turned to me but I spoke first. "Tell a story about Mom."

He shook his head. "I think we should talk about—"

"Tell the story about the lobster dinner," I said.

"Yay!" Bucky pounded the back of Dad's headrest. "The lobsters! Yay!"

"It was the first time you brought Mom to the Point," I said. "And she ran to the end of the yard and cried because it was so beautiful."

Dad hesitated. "Your mom was a great cook. She could make something good out of anything. She was also thoughtful. As a way of thanking us for having her, she decided to cook dinner. But Granddad insisted that we have lobster."

"Because midwestern girls don't have lobsters in Lake Superior," Bucky said.

"That's right." Dad's words sped up. "Granddad put the water on to boil and Mom pushed us all out of the kitchen while she made everything else. After about an hour, she said dinner was ready and we went into the kitchen to help with the lobsters. But she'd turned off the water under the pot, and the lobsters were gone from the refrigerator."

"Because Mom had taken them down to the dock and let them go!" Bucky yelled.

"You should've seen Granddad's face. He was so angry! But

Mom couldn't stand the idea of killing those lobsters. And all was forgiven, especially when Grandma and Granddad tasted her pasta. She made it from scratch. Just an egg and flour."

We passed the Pollards', then the Dennises'. I leaned out the window, smelling the pine and sea air. I smiled, thinking about Mom on the dock—dressed in her sundress, her hair blowing—setting the lobsters free.

Dad slowed, then stopped in front of the Debacle. Every light seemed to be on, but the shades were drawn.

"Go," I said. I'd been avoiding Allison. Had she told her dad about Ian and the drill? I glanced at Dad.

"Why'd you stop?" Bucky leaned forward.

No one moved. Then Dad sat back. "I saw your mom in my mind and it made me feel so . . . Oh, I *miss* her."

What would we do if he started sobbing and couldn't stop?

"It's okay, Dad." I patted his shoulder. He nodded and drove again.

Chapter 24

"Guess what?" Mrs. Steele said. It was Friday morning and Superior and I were back from a walk to town. The PT's car was parked at our cottage. Early. "A man called about the kayak. He's coming to take a look tomorrow."

"Oh. Are you sure you want to sell it?"

"Absolutely. Walt and I have no use for it anymore."

"Lucy!" Bucky called from our porch. "Dad wants you."

"Bye," I said to Mrs. Steele. Superior and I walked across the yard and into our cottage. Dad and the PT were at the kitchen table. She was dressed in shorts and a T-shirt and she wore those gold hoop earrings. "Hi," I said, touching my ears.

"We want to talk to you both." Dad smiled at her.

I sat at the table.

"Julia and I love each other very much," Dad said. "And, so . . . Well."

I pressed my leg into Superior, who sat next to me.

"Can we go camping on Upper Egg tonight?" Bucky asked.

"That sounds great. Are you up for it, Julia?"

"Sure. I love camping."

"We get these special hot dogs and roast them on sticks," Bucky said. "And we cook beans in the coals and eat them right out of the can! And we found really cool horseshoe crabs last time. Right, Lucy?"

"We can't go camping," I said. "We have a meeting about the Big House tomorrow."

"We'll be back in plenty of time," Dad said. "But that's not what we want to talk about. We want, well, we'd like to get married in January. What do you think?"

"Okay," Bucky said. Everyone looked at me.

I tried to see Mom's face, and when I couldn't, I felt my cheeks sting.

"How you both feel about this is important to me," the PT said. "I love your dad."

"I feel okay about it." Bucky took a big bite of his cereal.

How could he not *care?* I tried to list the things I didn't like about the PT. I couldn't. Because she was pretty nice and smart and all the things Dad told me she was. But I just didn't want her for a mom.

I got up, shoved my chair into the table and ran for my room, Superior close behind.

And this time Dad didn't come up and talk to me.

*   *   *

We left for the island late that afternoon, when the sun was still high in the sky but the boats had thinned in the bay.

We brought the usual gear: tent, sleeping bags, pillows, cooler and bags filled with food and drinks—including our special hot dogs, wrapped in waxed paper. We piled half of the things in the front of the boat, half in back.

Bucky and the PT sat behind me, laughing at Superior, who snapped at the wake. I hung on to my seat. The water was rough. When Dad looked at me, I forced a smile. *Mom would've wanted this.* How could Mom ever have wanted us to have a new mom?

Dad hit a big wave and the boat jumped before landing in the water. Bucky squealed, "Do it again!" I felt something filling up the achy, heavy space in my chest. It just kept filling, like a never-ending bucket of water.

"Lucy, we're gonna look for horseshoe crabs the minute we get there, right?" Bucky asked for the fifth time.

"Didn't I already say *yes?*"

"There it is!" Bucky yelled. I sat up straighter. We'd gone around Pear, and now Upper Egg grew in front of us, its shores covered with rocks and pine and birch trees. It was smaller than Pear and we hardly ever saw anyone else camping when we were there. Finally Dad pulled into a cove, out of the wind and rough water. We coasted to shore.

Dad wanted to drop the anchor, but it was high tide and he couldn't do it close to shore or our boat would run aground when the tide went out.

"This'll be tricky." He cut the engine and dropped the anchor. "We'll unload; then I'll take the boat farther out and swim in. Julia, you stay here and hand everything to us."

Bucky, Dad, Superior and I jumped. The water wasn't deep, only to our thighs. The PT handed us bags and we walked to shore. We set them on the beach, then waded back. The water was cold and full of rocks. Superior barked at us from the beach.

The PT wore her flowered bathing suit and a baseball cap. I watched as she bent over, lifted the cooler and turned toward us. But then she tripped. The cooler crashed onto the side of the boat, and everything inside spilled into the water.

"Oh, no!" Dad ran, water splashing around him. Bucky and I ran, too, only we couldn't go as fast as Dad. The PT jumped in, trying to rescue the food.

The Tupperware container full of fruit salad had opened and strawberries and blueberries floated next to our hot dogs. Bucky picked up the giant chocolate bar we'd brought for s'mores. The paper slid off and the chocolate slipped into the water. The eggs were smashed, the butter bobbed, a tomato floated.

We lost soda, jars of mustard and relish, and maple syrup. Bucky picked up ice cubes floating by him. Dad dove underwater and came up with two soda cans. I grabbed the orange juice container, half full, so it floated.

Dad and the PT burst out laughing. Hot tears filled my eyes. How could they think this was funny?

"Oh, come on, Goose, it's okay." Dad picked up a blueberry and squished it between his thumb and finger. They laughed harder. The PT's big mouth was open wide and water dripped from her baseball cap. I stomped up to shore.

"Lucy, wait," the PT said, laughing.

I whirled around. "You ruined the campout and now you're laughing about it."

She frowned. "I'm sorry. I'm clumsy when I'm nervous."

Nervous? About *what*?

"Nothing's ruined," Dad said. "We have plenty of food left in the boat."

"She ruins everything!" I screamed.

"Lucy!" Dad said.

"No, Ben, this is between me and Lucy," she said. "Tell me what else I ruin."

"Everything!" I couldn't stop screaming. "You come up here every weekend and now everything has changed and then you laugh about it."

"I don't laugh about everything." Her voice was softer. "I'm trying so hard to do this right, but you don't seem to notice. Or care."

"I care about a lot of things!"

"But you don't care about me. You're not the only one who has lost someone you loved." She started to cry.

Dad waded over and wrapped his arms around her. They held each other, the boat bobbing behind them. Bucky threw ice cubes. I felt numb. Then the three of them walked up to the shore.

"Let's just go home." Dad wouldn't look at me.

"Can't we look for horseshoe crabs first?" Bucky asked. "Lucy, you promised."

"Shut up about the stupid horseshoe crabs!" I yelled. "I don't want to look for them, now or ever! *Okay?*"

"Don't you dare take this out on him," Dad said.

"But that's all he talks about!"

"He's not the problem!" Dad's face was purple with anger.

"Listen, I know this isn't how you do it, but we'll make the best of it," the PT said. "Let's stay. Bucky, come look for firewood with me."

They started off for the woods.

"I'm not going to let *you* ruin the campout," Dad said, wading out to the boat. I followed and helped unload. Then he took the boat out farther, dropped the anchor and swam to shore. I stood on the cool sand and watched, miserable.

No one talked as we set up the tent and built a fire. I kept glancing at Bucky but he wouldn't look at me. Finally I felt something melt inside me.

"Come on, Buck." We started down the beach, stopping to turn over rocks, but all we found were blueberries washed up on shore. I glanced back at our campsite, where Dad and the PT talked quietly. "I'm sorry that I yelled at you. I'm just upset."

Bucky tossed a rock into the water. "Why do you hate Julia?"

"I don't hate her. I just don't want her for a stepmom."

"Why?" Bucky was on his knees, peering under a rock.

"I don't know. Why do you want her?"

"She's nice."

I wished he felt like I did. But he didn't remember Mom. He had nothing to feel guilty about. But then I thought, Do I?

Later we cooked cans of baked beans in the coals, then poured them into buns. They'd have tasted better with hot dogs, but they were okay. We roasted marshmallows, seeing who could make the perfect one—golden on all sides, but not burnt. Bucky won.

We talked about Dad's book, the PT's job and the Big House. No one mentioned what had happened. At the same time I knew it was the main thing on everyone's mind.

We cleaned up, then headed into the tent. It was huge, able to sleep ten. Dad and the PT went to one side while Bucky, Superior and I were on the other. We settled in and turned off the flashlights. I listened to the night sounds— June bugs hitting the tent, the breeze rustling through the leaves, water washing onto the shore.

Dad told us that he used to camp here as a kid. He'd always wanted to bring Mom for an overnight but then I was born; then I was too young; then Bucky came.

This was *our* tradition, Bucky's, Dad's, mine. Now the PT's. I glanced toward the other side of the tent but it was too dark to see. Then I remembered something the PT had said that day. *You're not the only one who has lost someone you loved.*

She'd lost her husband. Dad had tried to tell me other

things but I'd never wanted to hear them. Now I wondered. Had her husband died of cancer?

I didn't have to like her, but I shouldn't be mean.

"Julia?" My voice startled me.

"Yes?"

"I'm sorry."

"Thanks, Lucy."

And then I rolled over and tried to go to sleep.

Chapter 25

The Big House was packed. Mr. Ramsey started the meeting by reading a brief history that Dad had written.

"'Over the last twenty years alone, this room has witnessed numerous celebrations and arguments, a fistfight, one woman going into labor and a marriage proposal,'" Mr. Ramsey read. I glanced at Dad. "'It continues to be the heart and soul of the Point.'"

Everyone clapped. Then Mr. Ramsey talked about bonds. Inflation. Costs. Damage to the support beams. He turned the meeting over to Mr. Richards, who told us how long he'd been in construction and how many houses he'd built.

Ian, wearing a new lacrosse shirt, was back from camp and standing against the wall. Becca and Peter waved to me from the porch. I turned back to Mr. Richards.

"The shingles run straight into the dirt. That's one of the reasons we've got termites. Remember, the Big House was built for summer use, and these long winters are taking their toll. We'll have to do something soon. We shouldn't let another wet winter and spring go by.

"The southwest section has sagged because of the rotten beams. The easiest and least expensive thing to do would be to run an extra beam alongside the old ones and bolt them together.

"The next best thing would be to remove the entire porch; that way we'll be able to get to the other beams, see what shape they're in. What makes most economic sense, but only in the long run, would be to knock it down, start over and build it the right way."

"He's right." Mr. Pollard stood. "My brother's a builder and he agrees."

Finally everyone decided to remove the porch and see what was underneath the house. I sighed, relieved.

After the meeting, Mr. Richards stood next to the hole by the porch. I got on my knees and looked inside.

"Feel this?" Mr. Richards leaned over. I pressed the spongy wood. "Rotten wood, the same thing I found on our dock. The whole thing had to come down."

"Lucy!" Becca called. "Come on!"

We played chase long after the adults left. Several times I hid in my tree. Later, as we were on our last game, I climbed back up. Ian was there. We were quiet as I settled on his branch. Mosquitoes buzzed in my ears. Ian was so close that our arms touched.

"Your dad's a pretty good builder, huh?"

"I guess," Ian said.

I tried to think of something else to say. "Was lacrosse camp fun?"

"It was okay. But I'm glad to be back here."

We heard footsteps below. Allison stopped under the tree, the spotlight sending her giant shadow across the dirt. Ian climbed to the lowest branch, then jumped.

"Ah! What are you *doing* in a tree?" She didn't wait for an answer. "Look what I found in a closet at work. Leftover fireworks." She pulled a bottle rocket from her back pocket.

I dropped to the lowest branch and watched.

"And you just took them?"

"God, Ian! Relax. Here, hold one and I'll light it."

Ian backed up. "No way."

She huffed and emptied a soda can. She put it on the ground, stuck a bottle rocket inside and lit the fuse. It zinged up through an opening in the trees, exploding above us. I jumped to the ground.

Allison lit another. It shot into the leaves but didn't explode. We followed when she picked up the can and walked around the Big House. It was dark but a full moon and millions of stars lit the field.

"Do it again," Peter said as he, Bucky and Henry ran up.

We weren't allowed to light fireworks without an adult, not since Jake had blown off the tip of his finger with a cherry bomb two years earlier. What a terrible night. I knew I should tell Allison but something stopped me. Everyone crowded around.

Allison put a bottle rocket in the can and shoved it at Ian. "Hold this."

"No!" He stepped back.

She looked around. No one else wanted to hold it. She lit the fuse and pointed the can across the field. The bottle rocket would hurt her if it exploded in the can. But it shot out, skimmed the grass and exploded by the play structure.

"It's like a bullet!" Bucky said.

These rockets weren't as loud as the July Fourth fireworks. Still, I knew Superior was listening back at the cottage. Allison lit another fuse and pointed the can at the Big House. The bottle rocket zinged out, hit the side of the house and exploded.

"I bet I can get it in that window." She pointed the can at the window next to the door and lit the fuse. The rocket zigzagged before exploding on the porch steps.

I wanted to scream, "Stop!" But I was too afraid of her.

"Stop it, Allison!" Ian said.

She flicked her lighter in front of his face, the flame making his cheeks look shiny and red. "Big baby. Gonna go tell Mommy?"

Someone giggled. Allison kept flicking the lighter on and off in front of his face.

"Run home. Think Mommy'll save you?" Allison pretended

to cry, her voice growing louder. Lauren slid next to me, reaching for my hand. No one laughed now.

"Shut up." Ian's voice was low, angry. He glanced around the group.

"*They* won't help you. Your girlfriend already threw you under the bus."

Oh, no. I sucked in a breath.

"God, Allison, you're such a jerk," Ian hissed.

"Lucy told me that you broke Dad's drill. You're lucky I didn't tell on you the other night when Dad was complaining about it."

Ian glared at Allison. He'd really hate me now.

She lit another bottle rocket and pointed the can at us. "Run!"

Lauren screamed and hid behind me. Peter, Henry and Bucky dove to the ground. Ian smacked the can out of her hand and the bottle rocket fizzled out in the grass.

She slapped him, fast and hard, across the face.

Ian ran into the dark.

"Ian!" She took off after him.

The smell from the rockets lingered. No one moved.

"I wanna go home," Lauren said.

What had I done? I started for the road, everyone following.

"Did Ian really break the drill?" Henry asked.

"I don't know," I said.

"Then why did she say you told her?" Lauren took my hand again.

How could I explain this?

"Do you think she would've hurt the Big House?" Bucky asked.

"Nah, wasn't enough bang." I tried to make my voice light so they wouldn't worry. We passed the Grahams' cottage, the light from inside spilling across our feet.

"Why did she hit him?" Lauren asked.

"Because he wouldn't hold the can," Becca said. Everyone looked at me. I nodded, trying to swallow. Did Allison always treat him this way?

"Is Ian your boyfriend?" Lauren asked.

"No." And now we weren't even friends.

"Would Ian's sister have shot the bottle rocket at us?" Bucky asked.

"Nah, she was just trying to be funny."

"Well, she wasn't. She was so mean to him."

"I know." I felt my voice crack.

After we dropped everyone off, I walked Bucky and Henry to Henry's cottage, where they were having a sleepover. Then I started home.

Bucky's words pounded in my head. Allison wasn't just mean to Ian—she was horrible. In front of all of us. He must have been embarrassed. Angry. And I'd made everything worse by telling her about the drill.

I let Superior out, and we walked to the top of the dock stairs. The moon and stars had gone behind clouds and all I saw below me was a big black space. But I heard the water lapping the boats, docks and shore.

I'd been so sure Ian was a jerk that I never thought about the reasons he might act that way.

I felt as if I'd been turned upside down.

I glanced at the cottage. Somewhere inside, Dad was with the PT. I thought back to our trip to Pear Island, when she'd said, *There's always the other side of you.* Now I realized that she'd been trying to tell me something different from what I'd imagined. That maybe Ian acted the way he did because he was trying to feel better somehow.

I had to fix this.

I started for the cottage. It was so dark that I couldn't see Superior. I dropped to my knees and she was right there, licking my face. I wrapped my arms around her.

Through the windows I heard Dad and the PT talking. About me.

Chapter 26

"You were right, you know. She blames herself, more than I realized," Dad said.

"What else could she do? She was only six when her mom died."

"She couldn't get out of bed for weeks," he said. "It scared me. But I don't want her to feel so responsible all of the time. To—"

"Ben, you can't tell her how to feel. She'll feel what she feels."

Why were they talking about *this*?

I walked to the birch tree and slumped against it. Dad was the one who hadn't been able to get out of bed when Mom had died, not me. He hadn't been able to stop crying. He had scared *me*.

I tried to remember him in bed, but instead I saw the map on my ceiling and every nick on the chair railing. Then my head on the pillow as Superior ran toward me.

Was I . . . but . . .

Was *I* the one who couldn't get out of bed?

Now I really remembered Mom: her bald head and the circles under her eyes, the ugly cold sore in the corner of her cracked lips. I *hated* going to that hospital day after day. Feeling Mom's bony hip as I sat next to her on the bed. Staring at the black and blue marks where the IV sank into her arm. Listening to her heavy breathing as she slept.

Outside in the dark, I felt the big space open up inside me. Something like water rushed in my ears. Soon I wouldn't be able to breathe. I was so scared that I ran to the cottage. Dad and the PT were on the couch on the porch.

"I want to talk about when Mom died."

The PT stood and went inside.

I sat next to Dad. "It was hot. I wanted to go to a birthday party."

Dad nodded. "At the Rechts'. You and Katie were friends from preschool."

"There were balloons and a pool. I was excited because I wanted to go swimming." I couldn't talk fast enough. "And I remember a big blue slide."

Dad stopped nodding. "No, no slide. Tell me what else you remember."

"I wanted to go to that party, more than anything. More than seeing Mom again. And then I was sinking and I couldn't breathe and you carried me to the car." Something didn't seem right. "I was in the pool when you came?"

"No, you were in the house, having cake. I came to tell you about Mom. The minute I walked in, you knew, somehow. Maybe from the look on my face. You dropped to the floor and I picked you up and carried you to the car."

How had everything gotten so tangled up? "So my memories lied to me?"

Dad shook his head. "Not exactly. You were just so young. I think you thought Mom died because you left her and wanted to go to the pool party. Something like that."

No, Mom had died of a stage four glioblastoma. But something pinched my chest. This wasn't the only thing I'd gotten messed up lately.

I was so tired that I rested my head on the couch and closed my eyes. I didn't know what to think. I just wanted to sit here quietly while all this soaked in.

Then Bucky, in his camouflage pajamas, stood at the porch door. He held a big cookie in one hand, his World War II book in the other. Mr. Ramsey was behind him.

"I changed my mind about sleeping over." Bucky snuggled between us on the couch. Mr. Ramsey winked, then turned and walked away.

Superior sat up and put her head on Bucky's knee.

"She loves cookies," Bucky said.

"Don't give her any," I said. "Chocolate is bad for her."

"I know." Bucky took a bite of his cookie. "Remember the time she ate that chocolate cake and threw up?"

I nodded.

189

"You'd think she'd remember how sick she got," Bucky said. "I hate throwing up."

Dad and I laughed.

How far back did Superior's memories go? Mrs. Richards had lots of memories of her mom. Bucky didn't have any of ours. My memories were all jumbled up.

"Who wants sugar?" The PT stood in the doorway with a bag of cookies.

"Not Superior," Dad, Bucky and I said. We laughed.

Dad scooted over and the four of us squeezed together. I should have been angry that she and Dad had been talking about me. But I felt as if I'd confessed, let go of a guilty secret. Although I wasn't exactly sure what the secret was.

Julia broke a cookie and handed half to me. We sat, eating cookies and listening to the crickets chirping and bugs hitting the screen.

*

The next morning I walked over to Ian's house and rang the doorbell. Mrs. Richards answered. "Hello, Lucy, come in!"

"Is Ian here?" I asked.

"Out back." She led me through the house. Ian sat cross-legged on the dock, fishing. He wouldn't look at us as Superior and I walked up.

"What are you fishing for?" I asked.

"Bluefish," he mumbled.

I nodded and scratched behind Superior's ears. She closed

her eyes, happy. The water was still and calm, the sun dull behind gray and white clouds.

"I feel awful about what Allison said." My heart beat faster. "That night we played chase, I was in the tree and saw you take the drill out of the shed. But I didn't know for sure if you broke it. I shouldn't have said anything."

"Yeah, well, *thanks* a lot." He yanked on the fishing line.

"She kept asking me about what you're like in class. I was mad about the rubber bands at the marina and how you let your dad think that the kids broke his drill. Then, when she said you told your dad that I broke the rope swing with you . . ."

"I never told my dad that! Is that what she said?"

"Yeah."

He snorted. "She's *such* a liar."

"I believe you. And I'm sorry I told on you."

"I was gonna tell my dad, you know. I was just waiting for the right time. But Allison had to beat me to it. Typical."

"Was he mad?"

"Of course he was mad! Especially because of the tree swing, too."

"Both were accidents," I said. "They could've happened to anyone."

He scowled at me.

"You stopped her from shooting the bottle rockets at us. I just stood there."

"Ha! For once you didn't know what to do."

"You should've been at camp this week. The kids messed up the grass at the Big House. And I can't stop Peter and Becca's fighting."

"You gotta let them both win. They're supercompetitive with each other."

I nodded. He understood this better than I did.

He reeled in his line, then flung it back into the water. "Did you know Allison skipped a grade because she's so smart? She reads something once and *knows* it."

"One day she told us this stuff about raccoons that I'd never heard before," I said. "I didn't know how she remembered all of it."

"I bet she wasn't shy, telling you everything she knows. But she's usually right." He lowered his voice. "She thinks I'm an idiot. You think so, too."

"No, I don't."

He glared at me, then turned. It was low tide and patches of seaweed swayed just below the surface. Ian was lots of things. Impulsive. A big tease. But not an idiot.

"Just go away," he growled.

I sat there awhile longer, but he wouldn't even look at me, so finally I walked back up to the house. Mrs. Richards opened the door and I went inside.

"Any luck with the fish?" she asked. It was dark in the house, but I could see that her eyes were still full of rain clouds.

"Nah, not a bite." I glanced at the photos. My eyes had

adjusted to the dark, so I saw them clearly. Ian and Allison. Mrs. Richards. And her mom, standing in front of the light-house. I liked them, but if this were my house, I'd keep just a few on the wall. I'd spend more time outside, with the sun, grass, flowers, trees and water.

"I want to talk to Allison," I said. "Is she here?"

"No, she's working at the marina."

"Thanks."

Chapter 27

On the way to the marina, Superior and I walked by the Big House. Mr. Richards and Mr. Ramsey stood next to the porch, talking. I waved and Mr. Ramsey called me over.

"Know anything about these?" He held a handful of blown-up bottle rockets. "I found one of them on the porch."

If I told the truth, everything would change between Allison and me. I took a deep breath. "Allison shot a couple at the Big House."

Mr. Ramsey raised his eyebrows. "You know you aren't allowed to have fireworks, especially around the Big House."

"It was Allison, not us, and Ian tried to stop her." I turned to Mr. Richards. "The reason I didn't tell you about your drill was because I didn't know for sure if Ian broke it. I wasn't sure what I saw and I shouldn't have told Allison."

Mr. Richards frowned.

"But we all saw her shoot the bottle rockets," I said.

"Sorry about this, Joel," Mr. Richards said. "When I finish here, I'll speak to her."

"Okay," Mr. Ramsey said. "Thanks, Lucy."

I nodded and then Superior and I took off. The path through the woods was well trampled now. Above me the leaves on several trees had started to turn yellow. Soon, our summer up here would be over.

When I had first met Allison, I'd thought she was cool. I liked that she paid so much attention to me. Maybe she did that so she could boss me around. Maybe all along she'd planned to get something out of me about Ian.

My legs started to shake as I crossed the parking lot and looked in the store window. Mary was behind the counter. Down below, Pete was working on a boat. Then I saw Allison leaning over a dinghy on the last dock.

Once we reached the dock, Superior trotted ahead. Allison looked up as I stopped in front of her. A cleaning brush, rags and a spray bottle were at her feet.

"You're just in time to help." She pointed to the dinghy. "Can you believe this is what I have to clean today?"

I was afraid that I'd wimp out, so I didn't take my eyes from her face. "What you did the other night was awful, making fun of Ian in front of everyone. Then scaring us with the bottle rockets. And you lied. Ian never told your dad that I broke the swing."

"*Please.* You're just mad because I told Ian what you said."

"Maybe, but sooner or later I'd have figured it out."

"Oh, come on." She laughed and held out a rag to me. I crossed my arms and she frowned. "You're just like me."

I shook my head. "No, I'm not. And Mr. Ramsey asked me about the bottle rockets, so I told him and your dad. Don't try to blame that on Ian."

I turned and walked up the dock, shaking.

As the week wore on, I didn't see Ian. Was he still angry? And I avoided the marina. I wanted to talk to Kiki, but I was afraid of what Allison might have said to her.

By Saturday afternoon—the day of Jake's party—I couldn't stand it. I walked to the marina but Kiki wasn't working. Superior and I wandered back to the Big House. She'd have to show up sooner or later. I sat on the swing, kicking my legs under me.

A couple of weeks earlier, I'd sent my eagle drawing in a letter to Mrs. Jonas. Today I got a letter back. I took it out of my pocket and read it again. She told me about her summer, then wrote this: *I was happy to hear from you and hope we continue to write. Your drawing was magnificent! I'll miss you next year. The library at Taylor won't be the same without you! Please stop in and say hello sometime.*

What a great letter!

Just then Kiki pulled up to the Big House and got out of her car, paper bags loaded in her arms. "Hey, Lucy, could you give me a hand?"

I put my letter in my pocket and ran. I took a bag and followed her up the stairs.

"Have you seen anyone yet?" she asked. "They're supposed to help set up."

"No, I just got here. But I can help."

"Okay, thanks!" We moved the couches around the fireplace. I blew up balloons while Kiki set the other decorations on the table. I watched how she carefully hung the streamers, how she paused every so often to study the room. She was sure and calm and I imagined that this was what she was like no matter what she did.

She stood back and sighed. "Allison thinks this party is so lame, because Jake is turning twenty. But if my birthday was in the summer, I'd want a party here, no matter how old I was. Wouldn't you?"

I grinned. "The Big House is one of my most favorite places, ever."

"Me too."

"And so is the Point."

"Mine too." She smiled. "Maybe Allison would appreciate it more if she'd grown up here, like us. We're a big family, don't you think?"

Here was my chance. "Allison and I kinda had an argument."

Kiki laughed. "That wouldn't be hard to do. She's a little too cynical for me."

"And mean?" I watched Kiki closely.

She tilted her head. "Well, I just think she's lonely. You know? Anyway, don't worry about her. She went somewhere and won't even be here tonight."

"Where'd she go?"

Just then the door flung open and Danielle and Tonya hurried in, followed by Mr. Pollard and Mr. Ramsey. Everyone talked at once as they put drinks in the refrigerator and stacked food on the counter.

After that, I didn't talk much to Kiki—there were so many people around—but that was okay. She was right: we were family. And nobody seemed to mind that I hung out, helping, listening.

By the time Jake and his friends arrived, everything was set. I watched from the kitchen as Kiki and the others jumped out from behind the couches, yelling "Surprise!" Then some of the families stopped in to wish Jake a happy birthday.

When the cake had been eaten and the families had gone, Jake, Kiki and the others sat on the couches, listening to music and talking. Since it was just the older kids now, Superior and I headed home.

It was completely dark by the time we got back to the cottage. We walked to the edge of the yard and looked down. In the moonlight I saw Mr. Steele and a man on the dock, looking at the kayak. I ran up to Mrs. Steele, on her porch.

"Is that man with Mr. Steele thinking about buying the kayak?"

She nodded. "He called twice."

The Steeles' kayak was three years old, with scratches across the hull. *Such a beaut,* Dad had said when Mrs. Ramsey had paddled by in her kayak. But Dad didn't really care about new things. And a two-person kayak would be fun for all of us.

"I want to buy it," I said. "I started camp so I could make money to buy my dad a kayak for his birthday. I don't have enough to buy a new one, and yours is pretty great."

"Lucy, are you sure? It's a bit beat-up."

"I'm positive. I really want it."

"Well, I'd certainly love for you to have it but I feel funny charging you money. You're practically family."

I stood straighter. "No, I want to buy it. That's only fair."

"Let's get down there before Walt sells it."

Chapter 28

The next morning I found Ian in his garage, throwing a tennis ball against the wall. It was a good sign when he caught the ball and said to Superior, "Come here, girl!"

I smiled and nodded at her. She walked next to him and closed her eyes as he scratched behind her ears. I glanced at Mrs. Richards's car in the driveway, its trunk open.

"We just got back from my grandma's, up north," Ian said. "Allison's still there."

My grandma would have a whirlwind of things planned. "That's great for her," I said.

"You haven't met Grandma." He grinned.

"Oh."

"Thanks," he said. "For talking to my dad."

"It's okay." I didn't really want to talk about Allison anymore. "Guess what? I bought the Steeles' kayak."

I told him about how I'd started camp to make money for Dad's kayak. He listened as he scratched Superior's ears.

"So, now that you own it, let's go look for the eagles' nest," he said.

"Yes!" We took off.

Down on the Steeles' dock, Ian held the kayak while I got on. It tipped when he lowered himself; then it settled. Superior jumped on between us and we pushed off. We got into a rhythm quickly, our strokes matching.

The kayak bobbed. I glanced over the side but couldn't see the bottom, only cloudy water filled with patches of seaweed. My heart pounded and I shook the hair out of my eyes. Every inch of me felt nervous. Excited. Alive.

We passed the common property and the old lighthouse. It was hard to see the details of the shore from our speedboat. But now I saw how close the trees grew to the water's edge, how sparkly the rocks were. A long, fallen birch tree reached toward us, the underside rotting. I'd stared at this tree so many times but had never known what was underneath.

Superior tried to stand but kept slipping, so finally she just sat, watching.

My shoulders burned as we reached the end of the Point. The wind changed, blowing through us, and we paddled harder. We passed the rocks, and the water calmed. The beach was beautiful from out here, water rushing at the rocks, wind bending the tree branches.

We looked up. The eagle nest sat high in the elbow of a tree.

"It's gigantic!" Ian said. The nest seemed solid and strong, with sticks woven through it. But it was so exposed. How did eagles protect their young during a storm? "Are you sure the eagles are still there? Maybe they left the nest."

"They work pretty hard on their nests and come back to them every year," I said. We held our paddles across the kayak, staring at the sky and waiting.

Every day we met after lunch and took out the kayak. We didn't see the eagles, but we didn't tip over, either. Each day was easier for Superior, too. Sometimes I thought about how Annie might be with Ian—flirty, talkative. Then I'd get quiet, remembering everything that had happened between us.

But mostly we had fun. We paddled all over the Point. Superior and I showed him the path to town. And we caught stripers off the rocks at the beach.

The following week, Ian showed up on our last day of camp. Peter beamed and walked over to stand next to him. We played kickball and rescue princess and it was a lot easier with Ian helping.

At noon the moms arrived with cider and doughnut holes.

"To Lucy, for a wonderful camp." Mrs. Dennis raised her glass and everyone cheered. "Will you do this again next summer?"

"Maybe." Next summer I wouldn't have a kayak to buy.

"You and Ian could run it together," Mrs. Avery said.

"Yeah!" Peter said. Ian and I glanced at each other, then smiled.

After everyone left, I walked to Ian, waiting on the swing. "Thanks for helping."

"A lot of work." He laughed. "I'm glad it's over!"

We were quiet as we walked back to my cottage. School started next week.

At the cottage Dad made grilled cheese with Goldfish crackers inside; then the three of us sat on the porch and ate. Afterward Ian had to go home but we made plans to meet later. Dad and I watched as he started down the road.

"Mr. Richards stopped by," Dad said. "He's pretty sure the water damage at the Big House hasn't gotten any farther. Looks like we made the right decision, just to go after the porch."

"Yes!" I said.

"Ian's a good kid. Complicated, huh?"

I nodded. Would we still be friends when school started?

Chapter 29

Bucky and I hung streamers from the porch rafters. Kiki had given me the leftover ones from Jake's party. Then Bucky, Julia and I made Dad's birthday dinner while he sat outside calling, "What's going on? What are you making?"

The pasta wasn't cooked enough and the broccoli was cooked too much. But everyone liked the chocolate cake Bucky and I made. I kept glancing out the screen at the dark clouds. I couldn't wait to give Dad his present. Finally, after Bucky gave him a grenade made out of papier-mâché and Julia gave him books, I jumped up. "Come outside!"

"This is certainly mysterious," Dad said, following me. The air was cool and more leaves had started to change.

"Close your eyes." I led Dad to the edge of the yard. Ian and I had brought the kayak over to our dock.

We stopped. "Look down, on the dock."

He opened his eyes. "The Steeles' kayak."

"Not anymore. I bought it. Happy birthday."

"Whoa!" Bucky said.

"Lucy." Dad hugged me. "What a present! How? With camp money? You worked so hard. It must've taken every cent you made."

"It wasn't that much."

"What a thoughtful gift," Julia said.

"Thank you!" Dad said.

"What are you waiting for?" Julia asked. Dad grinned and took her hand, and we all went down the stairs. On the dock he put on a life jacket, then handed one to me. I gave it to Julia.

"Are you sure?" she asked. I nodded.

Bucky and I sat on the dock as they paddled toward the end of the Point. Twenty minutes later they were back and Dad climbed off, handing me his life jacket.

"Come on," he said. "We saw an eagle."

I yanked on the jacket and got on the kayak behind Julia. Superior jumped between us. We paddled, instantly getting into a groove. The water was rough as we rounded the Point. I looked over the side at the rocks and took a deep breath.

"Okay, this is where we saw it." She stopped paddling.

The sky was gray, and the wind strong, but the eagle nest didn't move. We were quiet. The water rocked the kayak. She turned to me.

"Did you know eagles mate for life?" This was the only thing I could think of to say.

"You know a lot about eagles."

She kept looking at me, so I said, "Did you know they

always come back to the same nest? And that they keep making their nests stronger?"

"They're good at remodeling." She laughed. I held my breath. I'd been trying to forget about what had happened on the campout. But I knew she hadn't forgotten, either.

"Lucy, remember when I told you that I knew what it felt like to lose someone you love? That happened to me. My husband died."

I swallowed. "How?"

"He had a brain aneurysm. Sudden."

"I'm sorry."

"Thank you." She nodded. "It was . . . awful. I don't think I'll ever get over it."

I didn't want to talk about this but at the same time I was interested.

"When I met your dad, we had so much to talk about. We shared this—losing my husband, your mom. Then I fell so in love with him. But you need to know something. You already have a mom. I'm not going to try to be a mom to you. I guess I'll be . . ."

"You guess you'll be what?"

"I'll just be Julia." She smiled and turned around.

I looked down at the water, tiny whitecaps peaking here and there. The water had been just like this the day we'd spread Mom's ashes off our dock. As the ashes bounced on the whitecaps and broke apart and floated away, I thought, Mom will forever be part of the ocean and the Point.

I glanced at Superior, her ears pricked, her nose close to the water.

Did people remember events a certain way in order to explain things? Maybe I felt guilty about Mom's death because I was trying to make sense of something that was too awful to understand.

"Lucy, look!"

An eagle soared high above us, wings spread. It circled over the water, then glided toward the nest, its head white, wings brown, massive, stretching the width of a house, it seemed. Its feet came down and its wings folded as it landed in the nest and disappeared.

"Wow!" I said.

"Spectacular!"

We smiled at each other and waited for another sighting. But the sky kept darkening and the eagle stayed in its nest. We paddled back. The water was choppier, but I had on a life jacket. Superior was here. The shore was close and Julia was in front of me, arms strong as she paddled.

It started to sprinkle when we reached the dock. We lifted the kayak and covered it with the tarp. The water rolled, black with whitecaps as it banged into the dock and shore. And then I felt that space open up inside me and start to fill with something heavy and wet.

I closed my eyes and breathed, deeply, slowly, as the wind blew through my hair.

I knew what that big space inside me was. It was sadness

and longing and something that had to do with losing what I loved most. It was my mom.

Then I opened my eyes. It was good to feel her this way, even if it was also painful. But she'd always be with me. And no matter what changed, nothing could take that away.

By the time we reached the cottage, cold, hard raindrops bounced off our shoulders, heads, arms—but we laughed.

"How about I make some hot chocolate?" Julia asked as Dad gave her a hug.

Bucky set up the Monopoly board and the four of us played on the porch, drinking hot chocolate and listening to the rain.

Chapter 30

My homeroom was in a science classroom, second floor. I sat on the edge of my seat, waiting for the bell. I wore what my friends wore: plaid shorts, T-shirt, sandals. I smiled and said hi to everyone. When anyone asked, I said, "Yes, I had a great summer! Did you?"

Three days earlier, after we packed the car, we drove around the Point one last time, stopping at the Big House. Workers had torn away the entire porch, and the house looked exposed, its beams and foundation open to the elements.

Dad said, "Think of it this way: the new porch will be much sturdier as it wraps around the Big House." Holding it, supporting it, protecting it.

Kiki stopped by on her way to college and hugged all of us. And I cried when we said good-bye to the Steeles.

The minute I got home, I called Mei, and we saw each

other that night. Mei, Annie, Rachel and I spent the last two days of summer together. Then we went to Duggan for an open house, and met the seventh-grade teachers.

After that we stopped by Taylor Elementary. Walking the halls and talking to our old teachers, who were setting up their classrooms, I was sad—especially when I hugged Mrs. Jonas. But Taylor felt small. And I could go back whenever I wanted.

Now Mei turned in her seat in front of me. She wore new gold peace-sign earrings. I wore silver. "Here comes Michael."

He grinned as he lowered himself into a seat next to Mei. So far, we were the only ones from Taylor in this homeroom.

Then Ian walked in and sat next to me. We smiled at each other.

Finally our teacher closed the door and everyone grew quiet.

"I'm Ms. Bruner, your science teacher. I've got your schedules." She was young, with short, spiky black hair and funky purple-framed glasses. She crossed the room and opened a window. Warm air rushed in, blowing her scarf over her face. She laughed.

I sat up straighter. Science might be interesting. She started calling names.

"Hey, Lucy!" Michael said. "Must've been a big bite seeing Ian all summer."

What had Ian told him? Mei rolled her eyes when I glanced at her.

Michael started in about summer camp and someone else interrupted with talk about baseball camp.

"Lucy." Ian leaned across his desk. "Did your dad like the kayak?"

"He loved it. He was totally surprised! And I saw an eagle."

"You *did*? Next year we're staying out there *all day* until we see one."

"What are you talking about?" Michael asked. "Your painful summer together?"

"Nah, it was a great summer," Ian said.

Michael hooted.

When my name was called, I grinned at Ms. Bruner as she handed me my schedule. Ian ran to the front when it was his turn. He took his schedule, then saluted Ms. Bruner. Everyone cracked up. Ian bowed; then she bowed; and then he bowed.

We laughed again. How he loved being the star!

The day before, I'd told Jenny about Ian and Allison and all that had happened. "Ian isn't as annoying as I always thought he was. He's got this other side to him."

Jenny bunched up her brows, serious. "You can't judge a book by its cover."

Then we cracked up, because that has to be the most overused saying ever.

But as I watched Ian, I remembered how Julia had said he might be covering up for something. I thought about how nervous she'd been up at the Point and how mixed up I'd felt when Mom died. Maybe there were all kinds of ways people acted to protect themselves against things that hurt or scared them.

Maybe everyone had another side.

Ian sat. I didn't know what kind of friends we'd be that school year. But the next summer we'd take out the kayak, look for eagles and share the tree during chase. Maybe we'd run camp together. Good things to look forward to.

Ms. Bruner finished handing out schedules.

Then she smiled. "Welcome to middle school."

ACKNOWLEDGMENTS

Many thanks to my editor, Wendy Lamb, and associate editor Caroline Meckler, for expert advice and bringing me back from the abyss. Thanks to Henry, Hannah, Herbie, and Bill and Heather Holmes Floyd for introducing us to paradise. Thanks to my supporters and readers: Susan Raskin Abrams, Jean Holmblad, Jane Malmberg, Pam McCuen and the other wonderful librarians at the Newton Free Library; Mordena Babich, Janessa Ransom and my critique group; Amy Jameson, Cynthia Pill, Susan Hurwit, Linda Gelda, Bryn Wood, Whitney Williams (dog extraordinaire), Dr. Stefanie Chin, Alison Dinsmore, the Balmuths and, as always, Kathy Read (the dramatic tension of closeness, wow). Forever love and thanks to the very best people I know, David, Dylan, Emma and Elizabeth.